Curvy Ever After:
Forbidden Curvy Girl Fairy Tales

By Twyla Turner

©Copyright by Twyla Turner

Cover by: Taria Reed Digital Artist
www.TariaReed.net
Models: Kevin Saldutti & Sharifa Edwards

This book is a work of fiction. Names, characters, businesses, places, events, and incidents are either the product of the author's imagination or used in a fictitious manner. Any resemblances to actual persons, living or dead, or actual events is purely coincidental.

To:
All the little girls that have grown up and became complete freaks! ;)

Table of Contents:

Preface

Three Wishes - Jazz & Apollo

Red — Red & Elan

Ashes - Ashland & Charlie

Bonita - Bo & Roc

Slumber — Ro & Flip

Yuki Shiro - Yuki & Cade

Wanderlust - Aliyah & Shayne

Acknowledgments

About the Author

Other Books by Twyla Turner

Connect with Author

Preface

These seven stories were a pleasure to write. And a nice break from the dark subject matter in the Damaged Souls Series. They are loosely based off of the classic tales we grew up reading and watching from *Disney* and *Grimm's Fairy Tales*. Their retelling coming straight from my naughty little mind. I wanted the heroines to better reflect the lovely curves of women around the world. And this cast of characters are just about as diverse as they come…a little something for everyone. Enjoy!

Three Wishes

Arabia 1244 A.D.

Jazz sighed deeply as she lounged on pillows and cushions made of Moroccan silks in bright and bold colors. She was currently listening to another of her father's tirades. Though, truth be told she was listening with only half an ear. They'd had this argument previously, several times in fact, so she'd heard it all before.

"And furthermore, you are the princess and *I* am the Sultan. You don't make the rules and you certainly do not disobey *me*!" Her father bellowed. "You *will* marry and to whomever *I* decide."

"But don't you care about my happiness, even a little bit?" Jazz asked. "I don't want to be some man's second or third wife. Why is it that men get all the spoils and women have to take it? To share like rabid dogs? I won't do it!" Jazz scowled and crossed her arms over her ample breasts.

"I'm done with you! You won't listen to reason." Her father huffed as he strode towards the door. He stopped then, and turned back, giving her a final warning. "You will marry. And it will be someone of my choosing. Otherwise, you'll give me no choice but to have you whipped." And with that, the Sultan disappeared through the double doors of her elaborate white marble chambers, in a whirl of the finest silks.

Jazz stared at the door in shock. Her father had never threatened to lay a hand on her. She knew she must have pushed him too far. In her anger and frustration, Jazz threw some of her pillows. The soft thump of the pillows didn't satisfy her need to break something. Finally, one collided with an elegant vase, shattering it into a million pieces. The sound only eased her frustrations marginally.

The princess knew she was running out of options and time. She didn't want to be a wife to some stranger she didn't love. Plus, she was already under her father's thumb, only to be immediately put under someone else's. Someone who may be cruel. Jazz didn't know why she couldn't choose who she was going to spend the rest of her life with.

She hadn't even seen another man, aside from her father. At least not that she could recall. When she was young she had been guarded by eunuchs. Though as she got older and prettier, even her father didn't trust the castrated men not to fall in love with her. So now she was guarded outside her chambers, but the guards were not allowed to look at her or step foot through the doorway. So only females were sent to attend to Jazz's needs.

It was like she was a prisoner in her own home. Next, she'll be a prisoner in someone else's palace. Jazz was so sick of the power men had over her, yet she hadn't even met any.

Jazz got up and slowly padded out onto her private terrace. Each of her steps felt weighted down with despair. The princess had no idea of her appeal, having been shelter all her life. Her generous hips swayed seductively. A hint of her solid thighs and the bare V between her legs, shown through the sheer fabric of her billowy fuchsia pants. Her butterscotch midriff was soft and exposed. Her full lush breasts were bound with matching fuchsia silk. The material wound around her back crossed over each breast and tied behind her neck.

Her beautiful ebony hair and stunning face remained uncovered since she never left her designated rooms. Jazz's hair was straight and thick, the ends resting at her tailbone. Only a gold chain with a pink jewel resting on her forehead, adorned her hair. Her face was heart-shaped with high cheekbones. A long, proud straight nose. Her mouth was wide and lips decadently full. And her amber colored eyes, under thick perfectly arched brows, were huge and round with a dense fringe of long black lashes.

Jazz's father wasn't a stupid man. He knew how gorgeous his voluptuous daughter was. So he kept her under lock and key. At least until it was time to pass her off to a husband that would then have to deal with her stubbornness and sharp tongue.

Jazz collapsed on a chaise lounge on the terrace. She tried to calm her emotions as the setting Arabian sun warmed her golden skin. Tears slipped down her face as she realized that she had finally lost the battle of wills for her freedom.

"It's hopeless."

~~~

Jazz unknowingly found the key to her freedom a week later. The Sultan swept into her chambers one afternoon, holding an ornate chest in his arms and smiling broadly. Jazz watched him walk towards her warily. His excitement never did bode well for her.

"Jazz, I have a gift for you. It's a chest of ancient treasures from your future husband, Ali Abdul." The Sultan said proudly as he sat the heavy chest down before her.

"What?!" Jazz exclaimed in a panic.

"I have arranged your marriage to the sultan of Baghdad. It's a good match." He informed her.

"For me or for the both of you?" Jazz asked resentfully.

"For us all, Jazz. And you will not defy me in this." The Sultan said firmly, brooking no arguments. "You will be married in a sennight."

"I hate you!" Jazz ground out.

"Hate me if you must, but you will marry him." The Sultan turned on his heel and left the room without a backwards glance.

Jazz picked up the heavy chest and with the strength born purely of rage, she launched it across the room. The chest exploded against the door that her father had just exited. The contents inside flew across the room in every direction. Jazz knew her father heard the loud bang but he obviously didn't care because he didn't come back.

The princess knew it was over, her fate had finally been decided for her. Jazz flung herself across her bed and sobbed uncontrollably. Eventually, she cried herself to sleep.

A couple hours later, Jazz awoke from a fitful sleep. She sat up in her bed and looked out through the double doors of her terrace to the evening sky, gauging how much time had passed. She sluggishly pulled herself out of bed. Jazz tried her best not to let the darkness of despair drown her. Though it was getting harder with each minute that passed that brought her closer to a marriage she didn't want.

She surveyed the mess she had made earlier that afternoon. She decided to clean up the chaos she'd created, needing something to occupy her mind. Jazz had to admit the jewels that were scattered around her room were beautiful. Necklaces, rings, bracelets, earrings, and headpieces in an array of colors, had been in the elaborate wooden chest.

Jazz crawled around on hands and knees, pulling the box along with her as she gathered up the jewels. When she was finished, she hefted the heavy chest up and gave the room a onceover to make sure she hadn't missed anything. Jazz's eyes landed on what looked like a gold teapot that had slid under one of her tables that were adorned fragrant flowers.

She walked over and picked up the pot. Jazz turned the golden teapot this way and that, inspecting it. She lifted the lid but she didn't see anything inside. She looked closer and on the side it looked like there was writing. Jazz rubbed her hand across it, trying to polish the gold to see if she could read the lettering better.

Suddenly the pot started to vibrate in her hands and Jazz dropped it quickly in fear. She watched as a white mist started to waft out of the spout. The vapor became thicker and before her eyes, Jazz watched as it formed into a man. A man that she assumed had to be the most beautiful man alive, since she had never seen one besides her father.

He stood quite a few inches over six feet. His body was massive, muscles bulging everywhere. Intricate tattoos accented the rises and valleys of his muscular frame. He wore only a pair of cerulean blue billowy pants with a thick waistband wrapped around his solid torso and wide gold bands around his wrists. His skin was a creamy brown. The man's wavy brown hair was pulled back into a ponytail at the nape of his neck. A dark beard ended in a point under his chin. His hazel eyes were lined with kohl, making them even more soul-piercing. Jazz was in awe.

"I am the Genie of the lamp and I am here to serve you. You may make any three wishes you'd like, mistress. And they will be granted forthwith." A deep seductive voice boomed from the giant man.

"Genie? Three wishes?" Jazz asked in disbelief.

"Yes, mistress. Genies can grant wishes to their owners. You only get three and you cannot wish for more wishes. So, chose wisely. Once your wishes have been granted, our time together will be done and I go to my next master." The man explained.

"And I can wish for anything that I want?" Jazz asked, excitement starting to surge through her blood. *Freedom!* She thought.

"Yes, mistress." The man bowed.

"Oh Allah, this is a big decision. I must think for a moment." Jazz said in a daze.

"As you wish," he bowed again.

Jazz turned her head to the side, looking at him thoughtfully. He stirred something in her that she had never experienced before. She wasn't sure if it was because he was the only man besides her father that she had been in the presence of. Or if it was because of the man himself. Jazz was also curious about how he came to be.

"Do you have a real name, Genie?" She asked.

"Yes, mistress. My name is Apollo." He answered with hesitation.

"Apollo." Jazz tested the name on her lips and tongue and found it pleasing. "The name suits you."

"Thank you, mistress." Apollo bowed slightly.

"You don't have to call me mistress. Please call me Jazz." She requested.

"Yes, Jazz." Apollo's voice rumbled deeply in his chest. The vibrations of her name on his tongue sent tingles to her most intimate places.

"Sit with me, Apollo. I need to think some more on what three wishes I want." Jazz gestured over to her elaborate sitting area. The large man followed her over to the bright cushions sunken down in the floor in a circle of colors.

Jazz eyed him across from her as he sat cross-legged, gazing at her patiently.

"Tell me Apollo, were you always a genie?" Jazz asked curiously.

"No, Jazz." He answered briefly.

"Where are you from?"

"Egypt."

"What did you do before you became a genie?"

"I was a palace guard."

"So why did you choose to become a genie?"

"It was not a choice." He answered honestly.

"What happened?" Jazz sat up straighter. *Is it possible that I'm not the only prisoner in the room?*

"Being a genie is a curse. A prison sentence." For the first time, Jazz saw a flicker of emotion pass behind his eyes. She wasn't sure but it looked like anger or anguish.

"Go on." Jazz coaxed.

"I was a palace guard to the queen. She found me attractive and pleasing to the eye, so she seduced me and took me as her lover. Even though I knew the consequences, she was a beautiful woman and hard to resist." Apollo stared off into space, obviously remembering the past. "The Pharaoh found out and my punishment was to spend a lifetime alone or in servitude whenever the lamp was found. Death would've been preferable."

"Oh my!" Jazz said in shock. "How long have you been a genie?"

"Centuries." Apollo said sadly.

"Allah, help you! Do you know of any way to be set free?" Jazz asked.

"It's okay, mistress. I mean, Jazz. Don't fret, I'll be fine." Apollo brushed off her question.

"No, tell me." Jazz pleaded.

"Well, I have to be wished free. But most people want to use their three wishes on themselves, not to release some lowly genie." Apollo said sadly.

"I will." Jazz looked up at him from under her long lashes.

"You don't have to do that, Jazz. I don't want you to feel obligated." Apollo refused the help.

"But I want to. I know what it's like to be trapped in a prison of someone else's making. I would see you free." Jazz said with a final nod of her head. "I'll ask for my two wishes first, then I'll set you free with my last wish."

"As you wish." Apollo said, his voice trying to remain calm. Though she heard the hopeful quiver.

The weight of his golden green stare made Jazz's heart pound. Her nipples hardened to little pebbles and her quim felt heavy with arousal. Her chest rose and fell rapidly as an idea for her first wish came to mind.

"Tell me, Apollo. Can you still be with a woman? Lie with her, I mean?" Jazz asked innocently. The relations between a man and woman had never been explained to the princess, but she had overheard her servants and maids discussing men. From the snippets she had gleaned, she still didn't understand the ways of love. Though she was desperate to learn before she decided on her second wish.

"No, I cannot. Not unless you wish it." Apollo told her.

Her decision made, Jazz sat up straighter with her chin raised high. "Then I have decided. Genie, my first wish is for you to be my lover, to take my virginity."

"As you wish."

~~~

Apollo watched as Jazz moved to stand in the middle of the bright cushion, awaiting his next move. It had been a least a century or two since he'd made love. More often than not, he was summoned by a man. He had figured that it was part and parcel to his curse. That was until he came across this beautiful and generous young woman.

Jazz was more beautiful to him than any woman he had ever seen. Before or after his servitude. When he had materialized before her, he had been instantly captivated with her beauty. Though, the reminder that he could do nothing about it, immediately filled him with sorrow. Now, it was like she was reading his mind. Her wish was his wish.

Apollo rose up to tower over her. His fingers clenched at his sides, wanting nothing more than to sink into her soft, luscious body. He reigned in his desire. He wanted to take it slow for her sake as well as his own. Apollo wanted to savor every inch of her. It felt like it was his first time all over again, and he didn't want to rush through it.

For the first time in hundreds of years, Apollo felt blood rush to his cock. He watched as Jazz's large doe eyes looked down at the tent his erection made in his pants. When she looked back up at him, he saw the confusion written on her face. And he realized that she was a complete innocent.

"Have you been kissed before, Jazz?" Apollo asked, his voice thick with arousal.

Jazz shook her head, unable to speak.

"Hmm…completely untouched then. I am honored." Apollo said gravely.

He raised his massive hands to gently cup her face. He stroked his thumb over her plump bottom lip. He gazed deeply into her wide eyes.

"I will show you all the ways between a man and a woman. Just follow my lead and you'll be fine," he instructed.

Apollo lowered his mouth to hers. He slowly swept his lips back and forth across Jazz's. She trembled slightly in his hands. He applied more pressure to the tentative kiss and Jazz remained tight-lipped, unsure of what to do. Apollo lightly nipped at her bottom lip and she gasped, gripping his wrists for support as he held her face.

He sucked her lip into his mouth and then let it slide back out slowly, from between his teeth. Jazz's trembles became stronger, her knees started to buckle and Apollo wrapped his rippling arms around her. He pulled her into his wide barrel chest as he deepened the kiss and gingerly flicked his tongue against hers. Jazz instinctively rolled her hips towards his. When she felt his erection against her stomach, she quickly pulled back and stumbled on the cushions, falling backward.

Apollo looked down at her sprawled against the colorful cushions. The sheer, turquoise silk and satin ensemble she wore, complimented her tan skin and left little to the imagination. He knelt down between her legs. Apollo's hands shook with want as he reached for Jazz's silk top. He tried to be gentle but his massive fumbling hands ripped it in two with one tug.

Jazz's eyes widened and she inhaled sharply as her breasts spilled out, into his rough warm hands. Apollo smoothed his hands over the outside curve of each breast, cupping them gently. His thumbs lightly stroked over her brown tipped nipples and he watched as they wrinkled and tightened to little candied drops, begging for his mouth. Apollo dipped his head down and hovered an inch above the hard nub. Jazz's chest rose and fell rapidly in anticipation. Not willing to make her or himself wait any longer, he tasted her skin with a flick of his tongue.

Jazz cried out at the sensation and Apollo grinned rakishly, as he continued his erotic tutorial. He circled his tongue around her nipple and then sucked it deeply into his mouth. Her hips rolled up to find him, in the carnal dance of need that she did not understand. And Jazz continued to writhe beneath him as he moved to the other nipple, giving it the same attention.

Her agitation grew along with the tension low in her belly. The lower part of her body was restless, practically begging him to come south. Apollo understood the language of her body, even though it had been years for him. So he kissed and nibbled down her soft rounded belly, dipping his tongue in her navel as he went. He passed over the waistband of her sheer pants and he could see the smooth, hairless V between her legs. Apollo bent down and blew cool air over her heated flesh and he heard Jazz gasp in response.

Apollo pulled her knees up and then gingerly spread them apart. He could see her sex glistening through the sheer turquoise cloth, smell her spicy fragrance. He closed his eyes and breathed her in, savoring the best scent in the world. *Woman.*

He lowered his head and softly kissed her bare mound through the silk. Jazz's hips jerked back in shock and he chuckled under his breath. Apollo loved that she was so sensitive and responsive. He knew they would work well together.

Apollo reached for the waistband of her pants and gradually pulled them down her legs, slowly building anticipation as his fingertips lightly raked down her wide hips and thick thighs. Once they cleared her feet, Apollo threw the garment to the side and they fluttered down to a heap on the floor. He looked back down at Jazz and his breath caught in his throat.

The image of Jazz lying there would forever be burned into Apollo's brain. Even if she didn't release him from his prison sentence, he'd keep the vision of her butterscotch skin amidst an array of bright colors for centuries to come.

Jazz looked up at him with wide trusting eyes. Her hair spilling out beneath her like a blanket of raven silk. Her breasts, full and heavy, spread before him like an awaiting feast. Her torso, soft and welcoming. Curving inward slightly only to flair out broadly at her hips, like the shape of an hourglass. The breadth of her hips sloped down to her solid thighs, protecting her untouched flower. Jazz's knees were drawn up and spread apart to display her slick jewel. Beautiful and pink, the custom to remove all body hair, leaving it naked for his viewing pleasure.

Unable to hold back any longer, Apollo clasped Jazz's hips and lifted her up towards his descending, greedy lips. His tongue stroked up her center as he drank in her sweet and spicy nectar. Jazz cried out at the intimate contact. Her hips shuttered, but Apollo held her close to his mouth, unwilling to relinquish her addicting flavor. His tongue flicked up on her swollen clit and Jazz grabbed a pillow and crushed her mouth to it, to absorb her moans of ecstasy.

"Apollo, please!" Jazz begged. "I-I don't know w-what to do!" She exclaimed breathlessly, pulling the pillow from her face.

"Let go." Apollo released her long enough to growl.

He quickly latched back on. Apollo used his lips, teeth, and tongue to torture Jazz to the brink and pushed her over the edge, into her very first orgasm. Her feet pressed into the cushions as she pressed up towards his mouth. Soft cries passed through her parted lips.

Apollo released her hips and Jazz collapsed to the floor but he was far from done. He stood and reached for the waistband of his pants and swiftly pushed them down his legs, releasing his turgid manhood that bounced stiffly with his movements. Jazz looked at his long, thick cock with curiosity, trepidation, and arousal.

"What is this weapon for?" Jazz asked.

"For pleasuring you." Apollo grinned.

"Does it bring you pleasure as well. Like when you put your mouth on me?" She stared at it thoughtfully.

"Yes." He answered breathlessly, imaging her mouth on him. "I too would find pleasure from your mouth on me."

Jazz sat up and shifted to her knees before him. Her lips were mere inches from his twitching shaft and when she looked up at him with big innocent brown eyes, he thought he'd embarrass himself by spilling his seed too soon. He clenched his teeth, trying to hold back.

"You can kiss it, swirl your tongue around the tip, or draw it into your mouth. Whatever you want. The choice is yours." Apollo instructed with difficulty.

Jazz thought about the things he had done to her body with his mouth and decided to follow his skilled tutelage. First, she placed a soft kiss on the angry purple head of his massive staff. The pearl of fluid seeping from the mushroom cap, smoothed on her lips and she licked it away with the tip of her tongue. Apollo's cock jerked in response to the seductive sight.

The princess opened her mouth and swirled her tongue around the head of his manhood and Apollo groaned. Spurred on by his sounds of pleasure, Jazz sucked him in deeply. His hips shook as he tried not to thrust into her wide mouth. She pulled back to breathe and stroked her tongue from base to tip, driving him to distraction. Jazz then wrapped her lips around him once more and slid down as far as she could go and Apollo pulled away before he lost his composure in her hot mouth.

"Enough," he said as she released him with a pop.

Apollo fell to his knees, clutched her face in both hands and crushed her lips to his. He held on firmly to her lips as he guided her back down onto the soft padding under them. He hovered over her, the tip of his cock at the ready at her entrance. His arms shook with the effort to hold himself above her.

"Our bodies were made to fit together. Like a sword in its sheath. Though there will be pain for you at first, I will try to be swift." Apollo forewarned the princess.

"I trust you." Jazz said bravely.

Apollo brought his large body down over hers and planted a soft kiss on her full lips. He positioned his thick shaft at her threshold and dipped in shallowly, stretching her muscles gradually. Her wet passage drew him in deeper and Apollo felt the barrier that symbolized her innocence and he drew back out. Poised at her entrance, he stroked his tongue into her mouth as he thrust through her hymen.

Jazz tensed in his arms and cried out against his lips, his tongue tasting her shock. Apollo pulled back and slowly pumped back in and she tensed once more but in pure pleasure. Once he realized she was ready, Apollo unleashed his full power. He slid his forearms under her back, wrapping his hands up and around her shoulders to pull her down as he thrust up. Their flesh met with a satisfying slap over and over again as his buttocks flexed during each powerful drive.

Jazz was lost. She lost sense of time and space. All she was aware of was the sounds of their bodies coming together and the grunts and groans rumbling deep in his chest. The taste of his lips, neck, and chest as she tasted his warm salty skin. Felt his throbbing cock deep in her recess and his hard muscles and smooth skin at her fingertips. Breathed in the scent of his spicy skin and sex in the air. Saw the passion etched deep into his face as he brought her closer to another shattering climax.

Apollo sat back on his haunches and pulled Jazz with him, onto his lap. He wrapped his strong arms around her, holding her still as he pounded up into her. Her next orgasm came slower but stronger than the first. Continual waves crashed over her and her womb rippled around him, squeezing his manhood tight. Apollo erupted, pouring his seed inside of Jazz. She gasped his name and he groaned hers as their breath came hot and heavy, mingling between them.

Jazz buried her fingers in Apollo's soft wavy hair, pulling it from its tie so that it spilled onto his shoulders. His hands moved from around her waist and quickly swept her long dark locks back off of her face, clutching the sides of her head and kissed her deeply. Apollo's body involuntarily pumped into her, his cock still rock hard after his explosive climax.

It had been centuries. He knew it was going to be a long night.

Later, Jazz lie asleep in Apollo's arms. He knew he had worn her out but he couldn't seem to stop wanting her. Needing her. He also couldn't sleep. He'd been asleep for decades and she had awakened him in more ways than one. And he worried what her next wish would be. He knew his time would be short with her, whether she set him free or not. A sadness he'd never felt, filled his chest painfully.

He gently caressed a strand of ebony hair off of her temple and she snuggled closer into the crook of his arm. She looked peaceful and beautiful as her long eyelashes fanned the tops of her cheeks, an occasional sated sigh escaping her lips. He leaned down and softly kissed her forehead, unable to stop himself.

Jazz's eyelids fluttered and she looked up at him sleepily. She smiled shyly and then stretched like a cat. All lazy seductress. Though she stopped in mid-stretch when she felt the evidence of his full erection against her leg.

"More?!" She said in shock.

"Only if you want. I would not force you." Apollo said slightly embarrassed.

"Is it always like this between a man and a woman?" Jazz asked curious.

"Not always. Though I have to admit that it had been centuries since I'd made love to a woman, so that might be why I'm still ready. Or maybe it's because of your wish. You asked for me to be your lover, so I'm ready when you need me." Apollo said, considering all angles.

"Well…since you put it that way, I definitely wouldn't mind it." Jazz lowered her lashes bashfully.

"As you wish."

Apollo quickly grabbed her hips, flipped her onto her stomach, pulled her to her knees and slammed into her already slick channel. Jazz screamed into a pillow as he wound a fistful of her silky locks in his hand, holding her still as he stroked deeply into her aching quim. It wasn't long before her climax ripped through her and her thighs quaked and turned to liquid. Apollo's release exploded, not long behind hers.

~~~

Jazz woke up the next morning and stretched her aching muscles. The pain in all the right places, reminding her of the best night she'd ever had. Her arms reached out on either side of her and she felt nothing. She quickly rose up on her elbows and looked around in a panic. The mattress felt cool to the touch, like Apollo hadn't been there in some time.

Afraid that he had somehow left her, Jazz jumped naked out of her bed and ran over to the lamp still on the floor. She quickly scooped it up and rubbed it vigorously. Once again, the lamp started to vibrate and the white mist poured out from the spout. Short seconds later, Apollo stood before her in all his gorgeous male glory.

"Apollo, I thought you somehow left me!" Jazz ran to him and he instantly wrapped her in his arms. Her heart was immediately soothed.

"I'm here. I just thought I'd try to get some rest myself and that wasn't going to happen next to you. I can't seem to stop touching you." He chuckled at the revelation.

"I'm glad." Jazz lifted her head from his wide chest and looked up at him smugly.

"I bet you are." He grinned reluctantly.

"I'm starving. I think I'll ring for breakfast and then get dressed." Jazz said as she slipped from the circle of his warm embrace and walked to the rope pull that singled her servants. "Do you eat?" She asked him.

"I don't need to, but I can." He answered as he took in her soft curvy form.

"Alright. We'll eat, and then I can tell you my next wish." Jazz smiled at him as she picked up the lamp again. "But first, I think you should get back in here. I don't want you scaring the servants half to death."

"As you wish, Princess." Apollo smirked before dissolving into the white mist and back into the lamp.

Once she was dressed and the large spread of food had been delivered to Jazz's chambers, she shooed the servants away and rubbed the lamp again. Apollo appeared before her and her heart fluttered like it did the first time. Though it was getting stronger with each time she saw him.

Apollo stepped up to Jazz and kissed her softly. "Are you ready to tell me your next wish?" He asked, anxious to find out what she wanted.

"Yes!" Jazz said almost breathless as she led him over to a table loaded with food.

Part of the curse was that he couldn't try to convince his current master or mistress to make a wish that would benefit him. The fact that Jazz had decided to set him free with her last wish had blown him away. No one had ever even asked about his circumstances that got him in the position of Genie. They heard that they got three wishes and they were off. Usually, with no thought to anyone but themselves.

Most people wished to be rich beyond their greatest imaginings. Some wished to cure sickness in themselves or loved ones. Heartbroken souls that wanted to bring back loved ones who had already left this world. Others wished for a hated nemesis to meet with hardship or even death. But the second most requested wish after money…love.

Apollo knew that Jazz was a princess, so wealth wasn't a factor for her. She didn't seem to be melancholy over a sick or lost loved one and she appeared to be healthy as a horse. She didn't seem like the type of spiteful person that would wish harm to anyone. So one of the only things he could think that she'd want, is love. Though for the first time ever, he prayed that that was not the case.

Apollo looked across the table at Jazz as she nibbled thoughtfully at her food. His nerves were completely frazzled and he couldn't take much more.

"Talk to me." He coaxed.

"Well…" Jazz sighed and then pushed ahead. "My life is not my own. It's been this way since birth. I've spent most of it in these rooms, not allowed to associate with anyone other than my designated servants. Until you, I can't even recall seeing another man other than my father. And now I'm told that I have to marry some man I have never met, in only a week's time." Jazz hesitated.

Here it comes…

"So basically, I want my freedom. I want the choice to be mine on who I spend the rest of my life with. I'm tired of men ruling my life." Jazz looked up at him from under her lashes. "Genie, my second wish is to have the freedom to make my own choices." She finished, looking at him meaningfully.

A slow smile spread across Apollo's firm lips as relief washed over him. "As you wish."

Jazz couldn't be too sure, but it almost felt as if immediately a heavy weight was lifted off of her shoulders. She felt buoyant and light, as if she could float away on a cloud of pure bliss. Now, it was her time to return the favor.

"Now…" Jazz paused for effect and Apollo held his breath. "For my last wish…"

"Yes, Mistress." Apollo said softly, thinking that this was the moment of truth. *Will she really be selfless enough to set me free?*

"I have wealth and now my freedom. There isn't much more I could possibly want. Except one thing…" Jazz stood up and came around to Apollo.

He turned to look at her and he sensed that he was about to get his hopes crushed.

"…but what I want, I can't have unless I do something first."

"And what is that, Mistress." Apollo swallowed hard.

"Genie, my third wish is to set you free." Jazz said softly.

Apollo stood up before her and the white mist that made him materialize each time she rubbed the lamp, swirled around him like a small tornado. Jazz took a step back as her hair whipped across her face during the torrent. Then the mist curled away from his body like a snake going straight to the empty lamp. The mist disappeared inside of the lamp and the bright shining glow the lamp once had dimmed. All its magical powers gone. The large gold bands wrapped around Apollo's wrist, suddenly clinked open and fell to the ground with a heavy thud.

The newly free man looked down at his bare wrists and then up at Jazz with wonder and a telltale wetness in his eyes. Apollo's throat was clogged with emotion and he couldn't speak to say thank you. So he quickly pulled her into his arms and kissed her hard and deep. His legs became weak with the realization that his life was now his own and he sunk to the chair with Jazz solidly in his lap.

He broke the kiss and searched Jazz's eyes. All he saw was joy written on her face and etched into her warm amber eyes.

"You actually did it. You set me free." Apollo said in wonder.

"Yes. Well kind of." Jazz smirked.

"What do you mean?" Apollo asked curiously.

"I wished for my freedom and then yours, so that I could tie you to me in another way for eternity. Oh, the irony!" Jazz's eyes sparkled with mirth.

"That's an eternity worth spending." Apollo grinned happily.

"What is the meaning of this?!" A voice bellowed from behind them.

Jazz looked up to see her father, red-faced and angry in the doorway. She stood up and took Apollo's hand as he stood with her. She faced the Sultan with her back straight and her chin held high.

"Father, I have decided that I no longer wish to marry Ali. I love Apollo and wish for him to be my husband." Jazz said firmly.

"Are you sure this is what you want? That he'll make you happy?" The Sultan asked.

"Yes father, I'm sure." Jazz said confidently.

"Well, alright then. Let the planning begin and the announcements made to public! Thank Allah, I thought you'd never choose." The Sultan grumbled as he swept out of the room in a flurry of fine silks.

Jazz turned to look up at Apollo, her wide eyes dancing with delight. He reached out and stroked his thumb over her bottom lip and she shivered in response.

"I command you to make love to me, husband." Jazz demanded playfully.

"As you wish, wife."

Apollo lifted Jazz into his strong arms and carried her to the soft bed, where he pleasured her for all eternity.

••••

Red

Jamestown, Virginia Colony 1610

"Now Rebecca, do not stray from the path to grannie's house. The woods are dangerous and the savages are always lurking about." Red's mother, Katherine, warned as she handed her a basket of fresh food and medicine.

"But mother, the natives aren't bad people. Didn't the girl, Pocahontas save John Smith?" Red asked perplexed at the hatred in her mother's voice.

"Well yes, but she saved him from her own father. Now don't question me. This is your first trip alone and I will not have anything happening to you. So do as I say and don't stray from the trail and talk to no one." Katherine said firmly.

"Yes, mum." Red said, contrite.

Katherine tied Red's scarlet cape around her neck and pulled the hood up over her dark auburn curls. The beautiful red cape draped around her cream white bodice, drab brown skirt and white petticoats. The cape had been a gift from her beloved grandmother and the nicest thing she owned. People had always been enamored with her dark red curls, but once she received the gift of the cape the whole town started to call her Red. Only her mother still called her by her given name.

Her mother saw her to the door and sent her on her way. There had been building tension in the colony between the natives and the newcomers. So everyone had been on alert, worried that the native people, the Powhatan tribe would retaliate for their land being invaded by the pale visitors. Red was surprised that her mother would let her journey through the woods alone, even though she was nineteen. But her mother doted on her, which was why she was the town spinster.

Red's grandmother had fell ill in recent months, so Red and her mother would often make trips to her home in the woods to bring her food, clothing, and medicine. But Katherine was too busy with the harvest to make the trip, so she sent Red in her place.

Red made her way to the mouth of the forest trail. A shiver ran down her spine as she felt eyes on her. She took a deep breath and brushed the feeling aside and stepped into the dense foliage. The tall trees blocked out the rays of the warm autumn sun and she was instantly enveloped by the dark, cool dampness of the woods.

Elan watched the plump, pale girl with the springy red hair and cape, make her way into the woods. His gold eyes glowed and his fur stood on end with attraction as she passed by. He could smell her sweet scent as the breeze ruffled her skirts and wafted towards him. He could hear her heart pound in her chest when a twig snapped in the distance. Entranced, Elan followed closely behind, just off the worn path. He felt it was time to introduce himself.

Elan quietly trotted ahead of the path. He shifted from his wolf form, his spirit animal, to his human body. He leaned against a thick oak tree as he awaited the beautiful girl to come into view.

Red rounded a bend in the road and her heart jumped into her throat at the sight of a man leaning against a tree. He was a native man. Though, as she eyed him warily, she realized he was a young man, possibly the same age as she.

His skin was stunning. A dark coppery brown. His dark brown eyes were deep set and seductive under raven-winged brows. His nose was straight and broad. His mouth, full and wide. And his hair was as straight as an arrow, jet black, and hung down to his waist.

He wore only tan buckskin leggings with a loincloth to cover his private bits in the middle and moccasins. His upper body was bare. His shoulders were broad and square. His muscles were lean in his tall frame. To Red, he seemed to have the wildness and raw power of an animal. He was the most beautiful man she had ever seen.

Though his beauty didn't block the wariness that had settled into her stomach. Red realized that she had stopped to stare at him, as he stared back at her. She quickly started walking again, increasing her pace and gripping her basket tightly. As she passed him, he pushed off of the tree and fell into step beside her. Red's heart thumped in her chest like the beating of a steady drum.

"Hello." He said deeply, surprising Red that he could speak English. "I am Elan." He said haltingly as if he were testing the new language on his tongue.

"I shouldn't be talking to you." Red said quietly as she tried to walk faster.

"Why?" Elan asked with a raised brow, easily keeping pace with her.

"B-Because my mother told me not to talk to anyone and to just head straight to my grandmother's house." Red explained, giving away too much.

"Do you do everything your mother tells you?" Elan smirked at her.

"Well, of course."

"Listening to your mother might make you miss out on a world you never knew existed. I promise, I'm nice. My name even means 'friendly' in my native tongue." Elan coaxed, a huge beautiful smile spread across his face, showcasing stunningly white teeth.

Red was mesmerized. He really did seem harmless. *And beautiful. Definitely, beautiful.* Red thought to herself.

"Alright." Red said, blowing out a huge breath as she took a chance. She held her pale hand out to him and his reddish brown hand clasped hers warmly. She instantly felt a charge of electricity shoot up her arm. "I'm Red. Well, Rebecca actually but everyone calls me Red."

"You are beautiful, Red. I've never seen skin as fair as yours or hair so fiery and curly. What are these spots?" Elan asked, pointing to her face near her nose.

"Oh, my freckles? Yes, I hate them." Red said sadly about the tiny dots that dusted her cheeks and nose.

"Freckles." He tested the new word on his tongue. "No, they are lovely." Elan said sincerely.

Red flushed prettily, her cheeks turning a bright pink.

"So why are you visiting your grandmother this day?" Elan asked curiously.

"She is sick. So I'm bringing her food and medicine." Red told him, feeling more at ease with each passing moment in his company. He had a calming presence.

"I am so sorry to hear that." Elan apologized.

"It's okay. Thank you for your concern." Red sighed heavily. "Well, I must be going. It was lovely talking with you, Elan." Red continued down the dirt trail.

"Why must we part ways? I'd like to continue talking with you. It's so very rare that I get to use my English." Elan told her.

"I don't think it's a very good idea." Red looked at him and the attraction she felt coursed through her body. *Mother would not be pleased.*

"But I do. Besides, I haven't had a chance to kiss you yet." Elan said boldly, looking directly in her deep blue eyes.

Red's breath hitched in her throat. "I-I'm afraid that wouldn't be p-proper," she whispered.

"Don't be afraid. Come." Elan reached for Red's hand and guided her deep within the woods.

Red knew she should pull away and run back to the main road, but it was as if she was under a spell and she followed willingly. Elan led her to a large tree and spun her around till her back rested against the rough bark. He stepped closer to her and his mouth hovered only a half an inch from hers. Red closed her eyes and lifted her mouth to him, excitement running through her veins. Many boys and men had looked at her with lust in their eyes but under her mother's watchful eye, she was never able to get close to anyone.

Elan placed a long finger against her pink pouty lips. "I didn't mean here." He lowered his hand to her full skirt and petticoats. "I meant here."

"Dear God." Red gasped and dropped her basket to the ground. She was scandalized, yet the temptation kept her from saying no.

Elan's hand traveled from her lips to her chin and neck. His fingertips danced over the swells of her creamy alabaster breasts to the laces of her bodice. He made quick work of unlacing the fabric and pulling it down along with her skirt. He untied her petticoats and they fell in a heap at her feet. Eventually, Red was left in nothing but her cape, white cotton shift, thigh-high stockings and leather shoes.

Red's chest rose and fell rapidly in anticipation. She watched as Elan unlaced the ties of her shift and with a gentle brush of his hands, the material fell away. She was left bare and on display, her cape hiding nothing but her hair. He then pushed back her cape, wanting to see all of her wild red curls.

Elan stepped back and took in her tall, ripe, and voluptuous beauty. Her soft curves were flawless ivory. Her heavy breasts tipped with tiny pink nipples. The apex of her legs, a triangle of fiery red. Her sapphire eyes, bright with longing.

Red saw the look of desire on his face as he took in her naked body. She noticed that his loincloth no longer laid flat against his thighs but tented out before him. She had heard the whispered conversations of married women and knew that it was a sign that he wanted her.

Elan moved close to her once more and slowly sunk to his knees in front of her. He clasped each of her feet and removed her shoes, one at a time. He unhurriedly slid his hands up her stocking clad legs. Once he reached her thighs, he gently pushed them apart, exposing her pale pink nether lips. He placed a soft kiss on her springy red mound. Craving her taste, Elan wrapped his lips around her pretty lips and lapped at her slit. He tongue stroked up and then swirled around her distended clit.

Red gasped and pulled her hips away from his mouth at the same time that she pushed his head away. Never in all her life, had she felt anything so amazing. She had been unprepared for the heady feeling.

"Do you want me to stop?" Elan asked as he looked up at her, his lips wet with her arousal.

"No! Kiss me some more!" Red panted.

He quickly obliged her and latched back onto her throbbing cunny. Red bucked wildly against his hungry mouth and her fingers tangled in Elan's long ebony strands. He reached up and stroked the folds of her lips, playing at her slick entrance with his fingertips. He slipped a long finger into her heat and her tight untouched walls created suction around the one digit, pulling him in welcomingly. Elan began to slide his finger sensually in and out of her wet cleft as he curled his tongue around her swollen pearl.

Red rolled her hips, creating more friction against his eager mouth. Something in her tummy fluttered and gained speed as she pumped faster astride his tongue and finger. The flutters turned into a ball of tension and with a flick of his tongue and a curve of his finger, it exploded. Feminine cum rushed from her slit and splashed against her thighs and his awaiting mouth. Red wailed her release, only the woodland creatures were close enough to hear.

Elan draped her left leg over his shoulder and stood quickly, spreading her quim. He swept his loincloth aside, baring his thick stiff cock. He plunged into her deep recesses and tore through her maidenhead without warning. Red gripped his shoulders and screamed. Elan finally brought his lips to hers and devoured her mouth. She tasted her savory flavor on his tongue, never imagining her first kiss would be like this.

The pain of her hymen being breeched subsided and as Elan continued to stroke into her taut passage, the friction created delicious sensations. Every inward thrust hit a sensitive spot deep in her womb that made her thigh quiver each time. Elan leaned further into her, bringing her leg that rested on his shoulder, flush against her chest. He reached out and grabbed the tree that was holding her up as leverage and his powerful lunges increased. The slap of his flesh against hers and Red's cries were the only sounds in the forest. As if the woodland creatures had silenced their chatter to the sensual symphony happening amongst them.

Elan's mouth moved from her small, pouty lips to her chin and neck. His copper hand cupped her creamy alabaster breast, lifting the tiny pink peak to meet his lips. He swirled his tongue around the hardened tip and flicked it as he thrust forward and Red shattered. The leg that still held her up shook uncontrollably. Her inner walls rippled and squeezed his pumping shaft.

As the beautiful native man continued to pummel her flesh, drawing out another climax from her, Red heard him begin to chant something in his language. Her heavy-lidded eyes watched as his silky hair fell across his handsome face. He continued speaking in a tongue she didn't understand and she saw his chocolate brown eyes flash to gold and then back again as rapture overtook him. Elan shouted out his release and he held completely still. Red felt his cock throb inside of her as he spilled his seed deep within her.

They both crumpled to the ground. Red's skirts and petticoats cushioned their fall. They both fell into a sated sleep, wrapped in each other's arms.

~~~

An hour later, Red's eyes slowly opened. She looked up at the green canopy of the treetops above, just a hint of blue skies peeking through. She slowly looked to her right where Elan had been, but he was gone.

Red stood and began to dress, a sadness filling her heart. She had no idea how or when she'd see Elan again. Once she was dressed, she started back towards the path to her grandmother's house. With no distractions and her mind preoccupied with thoughts of Elan and his passionate lovemaking, it didn't take her long to reach the small cottage.

Red opened the front door and peeked her head inside. "Grandma, it's me Rebecca."

She opened the door fully and stepped inside. There were no signs of her grandmother anywhere. The only signs of life in the home was an odd snow white owl perched on the post of her grandmother's bed.

"Well you're not my grandma." Red said, coming close to the bird.

She held out her arm and the owl spread its pristine wings, lifted off of the post and landed on Red's extended arm. She looked at the bird closely, the feeling that it looked at her with recognition came over her. Red shook off the silly notion.

"You have such big eyes," she said to the bird and it blinked in response. "With such a large pointy beak and big talons."

A noise from a dark corner of the cottage drew Red's eyes. What she saw nearly stopped her heart. The gold eyes of a wolf stared back at her. It slowly stepped out of the shadows and Red backed up, but the small kitchen table stopped her progress. She watched in terrified fascination as the wolf morphed into the form of a man crouched before her. The man unfolded his body as he stood up and Red gasped when she realized that it was Elan.

"Elan! W-What *are* you? Why are you here? And what d-did you do to my grandmother?" Red began to panic.

"Hello, Red." Elan said calmly. "I'm a shifter. The wolf is my spirit animal. I'm here to save your grandmother from sickness. And you're grandmother is currently sitting on your arm." Elan answered each of her questions in order.

"What?!" Red cried, looking at the owl in shock.

The owl flapped its wings and flew off of Red's arms and in midair transformed into her grandmother. Red's mouth flapped open and closed several times. She was unable to form words for the things she had just seen.

"Don't worry, dear. I'm alright." Her grandmother soothed. "This wonderful young man told me that he met you along the path and that you told him of my illness. So he came straight away to come heal me. Says his father is a medicine man and showed him the ways of a healer," she explained.

"So you turned her into a bird?!" Red shouted at Elan.

"I'm alive and healthy, am I not?" Her grandmother said with hands on her hips.

"Well...yes but-"

"Well, but nothing. Stop your fretting. I've never felt better." Red's grandmother grinned brightly.

"The owl is her spirit animal. To embody your spirit animal, is to embody life." Elan informed Red.

"Your mother shelters you too much. She thinks the natives are savages but I think some of their customs are quite extraordinary." Her grandmother said as she patted Elan's arm affectionately.

"Yeah, I've experienced some of them." Red raised a fiery brow at Elan.

Elan had the grace to blush. "I could not resist. I had to have you. I apologize for being so forward. But it doesn't matter now, we have mated before Mother Earth. We are now one. Joined forever."

"Does that mean we're...*married*?" Red asked astounded.

"For the most part. Now you can embody your spirit animal too." Elan told her.

"*My* spirit animal?"

"Yes. You are a fox. Red and curious." Elan grinned.

Red turned to her grandmother. "And you're okay with this, Grandma?"

"Dear, if there's one thing I've learned in my advanced years, it's that if you are lucky enough to find a gorgeous man that kisses the ground you walk on...keep 'em!" Her grandmother winked at her conspiratorially.

Elan held out his hand for Red to take. She looked at his face, warm and welcoming. She reached across the distance between them and took his hand, taking the first step into the unknown with an open mind and heart.

When her hand touched his, she closed her eyes and felt the world fall away. Red opened her eyes again and Elan was once more in his wolf form. She realized that she was on all fours. She looked down to see two little red paws and she quickly glanced back to see her furry red hindquarters and white tipped fluffy tail. Red looked up at her grandmother standing above them.

"Go." Her grandmother encouraged, happily.

Red and Elan took off out the open door into the wilderness. She felt wild and free as she chased after Elan. That's when Red realized that though her mother had given her sound advice, not everyone's path was the same. Not every stranger was dangerous. Her life was meant to be an adventure and it was time to carve her own trail.

••••

Ashes

Once upon a time in a city far, far away…
Alright, it was New York, so maybe not that far.
There was a beautiful, plump, dark-skinned beauty named Ashland. Her father had been the head of a major entertainment magazine La-La Land, and her mother had died during childbirth. At a still tender age, Ashland's father remarried to a pinched faced woman named Ester. Who had two tall, willowy, gorgeous twin daughters, Sophia and Olivia.

At first, Ester and her daughters were kind to Ashland, if not slightly aloof. The girls snickering behind her back when they thought she wasn't looking. Though, tragedy struck the household when Ashland's father collapsed and died of a heart attack one year after marrying Ester. Immediately following his death, their true cruel selves were finally revealed. And Ashland quickly realized that the trio had souls as evil as the devil's own heart.

Ester took over as CEO of La-La Land magazine, she turned the once respected entertainment magazine into nothing more than a filthy tabloid rag. She made Ashland into little more than her and her daughter's personal servant, in her father's expansive penthouse apartment. And Ester's horrible daughters made it their job to turn Ashland's life into a living hell.

Her smooth, dark skin was looked down upon in comparison to their caramel-colored skin. So they called her ugly because of her dark mahogany skin. To add insult to injury, her short, round plump body in juxtaposition to their long slender frames, gave them more fodder to torment her. Every large animal that they could compare her to, they would. Things certainly didn't improve when they both became models, as they threw their exalted beauty in her face. Last, but certainly not least, they called her Cinderella. They said that her name was the perfect fit for the role of a servant. And if they didn't call her Cinderella, they'd call her Ashes.

Ashland knew that though her life was similar to the storybook character in many ways, it was highly doubtful that she'd have the same storybook ending. She knew that there would be no prince to come to her rescue and get her out of her pathetic situation. Though, in high school she found the key to her freedom. On a day that her stepmonster and evil stepsisters were out shopping, she went through her father's things and found his old camera. It was the camera that opened doors to him in the magazine business as a photographer. In his later years as a CEO, he didn't have much time to take beautiful photographs. So he put away his old camera and forgot about his cherished hobby.

Picking up the camera and his beloved pastime, Ashland found solace behind the lens. And so began her passion for taking stunning pictures. It was her unique photos and vision that got her recognized by colleges and universities and landed her a scholarship to the Art Institute in NYC. During her time there she was blessed enough to make connections with her father's old colleagues and found an amazing internship at a fashion magazine. By the time she graduated from the Institute, she had built up quite a good reputation as a phenomenal, up and coming fashion and editorial photographer.

Ashland quickly, yet regretfully moved out of her childhood home the moment she graduated. She moved into a tiny flat in Soho with her newly popular designer best friend, Francisco Cortez. He was Latino, gay, and utterly fabulous. Together, they were trying, quite successfully, to conquer the fashion world with trendy and flattering plus-size clothing combined with high fashion photography.

At the moment, Ashland was helping Cisco with some last minute adjustments on his new fall collection that would be featured on New York Fashion Week's runway the next day. He was a bundle of nerves and extra bitchy. Especially, because she was leaving him soon to help her stepfamily with some Fashion Week festivities.

"I can't believe you're leaving me to go help the wicked witch of the west and her two evil flying monkeys," Cisco pouted prettily. His lips a sparkling pink from his shimmery lip gloss.

He was tall and slender with a sleek, slicked down hipster haircut. His long limbs were encased in a tight-fitting t-shirt with Marilyn Monroe on the front of it and black hip hugging skinny jeans.

"I know. I know," Ashland sighed. "I should tell them to kiss my big ass, but I'm such a wuss when it comes to telling them no."

"You don't have to tell them no, honey. Just ignore the phone calls or let me answer the phone. They'll never ask you for anything ever again after I'm done with those bloodsucking primadonnas," Cisco finished indignantly. His perfectly arched eyebrows raised high.

"I really should. Maybe next time," Ashland said, trying to pacify him.

"Sweetie, you say that every time." Cisco patted her hand sympathetically. "It's time you start standing up for yourself."

"Okay, okay. I'm not in the mood to hear this self-love lecture again," Ashland said angrily, pulling her hand away from her best friend. "When I find my spine, I'll let you know," she growled in frustration.

Cisco's head snapped back and his eyes widened as he nodded his head proudly. "I think you just did."

Ashland audibly groaned, instantly feeling bad for lashing out at the one person who meant the world to her. "I'm sorry, Cisco. I didn't mean to snap at you. You know how discombobulated I get before I see them." She blew a harsh breath through her bare lush lips, her breath fluttering her jet black bangs on her forehead.

"Don't worry about it. I liked it. I like you all smart-mouthed and sassy." He winked at her. "So I'll see you tonight at the ball?"

"Yep. Just remember, I'm not there to have fun. I'm there to work. I'll be behind the camera, just the way I like it. Snapping pics of you beautiful people. Except with shoes on." Ashland reminded him. Sighing at not being able to take pictures barefoot like she was used to. It was her odd habit. The moment she picked up her camera at a photo shoot, she'd kick off her shoes like Patti LaBelle at a concert. But that wouldn't be appropriate at a formal ball.

"Oh please, honey. One day I'm gonna pull you out from behind that damn camera. You need to show the world how beautiful *you* really are," Cisco said with conviction.

"Oh yeah, right." Ashland scoffed. "The majority of the world does not consider 'round and dark brown' beautiful."

"Then it's our job to show them how wrong they are," Cisco said, looking her soft, curvaceous body up and down. Hidden behind a shapeless dress, long scarf, and knee high brown boots. "I can't wait for the day you let me play dress up. A little makeup here. A new hairdo there. Some of my amazing designs accentuating this knockout body, and…BAM, you'll have men lining up for miles. And maybe then, you'll finally have the confidence to get naked and pop that damn cherry!" Cisco finished with a smack on her substantial behind.

Ashland yelped in surprise and then gave him a cutting look. "Keep your hands to yourself, perv. Whether my cherry is still intact or not, is none of your business. And the day you dress me up like some doll, is the day pigs fly outta my ass." Ashland scowled at him before she grabbed her brown leather camera bag that also doubled as her purse. She flung the long strap around her body, letting it rest in its usual spot on her shoulder, giving her a sense of comfort. "I'll see you later at the ball." She smirked at her best friend and gave him a quick kiss on the cheek before leaving his design studio and heading to the Upper East Side.

~~~

"You're late, Ashes." Olivia snapped as Ashland stepped through the front door.

Not feeling up to being berated, Ashland uncharacteristically spoke her mind before she knew what she was saying. "It's not like I'm exactly on the payroll. I'm helping as a favor, *not* as your slave. Be glad I'm even here."

Sophia gasped on her sister's behalf. "Do you know who you're speaking to? You don't talk to us like that."

"You're only where you're at because my father married your mother and left everything to her when he died. *My* father's generosity and blindness got you here. Nothing else," Ashland said, her teeth gritting.

"You're a bitch!" Olivia shouted at her.

"We'd still be models whether your father married our mother or not. That's what happens when you're tall and beautiful. Unlike short, fat trolls like you." Sophia said snidely, looking up from her perfectly manicured nails.

Tears stung the back of Ashland's eyes. The same tears that always came when she heard certain trigger words that catapulted her back to all the years of torment they had inflicted upon her. She blinked rapidly a few times, stifling her tears. She never wanted them to see her break.

"You know what, I'm not here to fight. What do you need help with?" Ashland sighed deeply.

"That's better," Olivia said with contempt. "We need you to help decorate the house for the pre-party before the masquerade ball, while we get ready for the evening."

"Didn't you have all day to decorate?" Ashland asked, irritated with their laziness.

"All the decorations are lined up there," Sophia said, ignoring her question. Then she pointed over at the bags and boxes lining the wall that seemed to stretch on for days.

"Fine. Whatever," Ashland said, turning her back on them. Dismissing them.

As they left the living room and headed back towards their bedrooms, Ashland's stepmother swept into the room. Her face pinched as usual.

"Oh Ashland, you're finally here," Ester said, looking her up and down like a disgusting bug that needed to be squashed. "My…my, we've packed on a few pounds, haven't we? Well, you never were a great beauty. Thank goodness for your little career you've got going for yourself."

"Yes, because being beautiful is so much more important than being kind, intelligent and a decent person in general," Ashland said between clenched teeth.

"Are you suggesting something, dear?" Ester asked with a raised brow.

"I wouldn't dare, stepmother." Ashland challenged.

"Good. You'd do well to remember that with one phone call, your career would be over. You only have a career because I allow it." Her stepmother threatened.

"Yes, ma'am." Ashland bowed her head in defeat.

"I'm glad we understand each other. Now, hurry up and get these decorations up. Our guests will be arriving in a couple of hours." She commanded, before turning and gliding into the kitchen to oversee the progress there.

Ashland quickly swiped at a few tears that had escaped down her cheeks with the back of her hands. She walked over to the wall of packaged decorations and took a deep breath, before getting to work.

~~~

A couple of hours later, Ashland was just finishing up the garish decorations when Sophia and Olivia glided into the living room. They were resplendent in elegant ball gowns. One in pale pink and other in green pastel. Which, unfortunately complimented their creamy caramel coloring to perfection.

Ashland was throwing the strap of her camera bag over her shoulder, getting ready to leave when Sophia stopped her.

"Oh my goodness! I'm so forgetful. Ashes, I forgot to tell you that I signed you up to attend the ball as a guest, not as a photographer. Oops." Sophia finished with a sly smile.

"Wait. What?!" Ashland said, panicked. "I don't have anything to wear to actually attend the ball as a guest."

"Well, that sucks," Olivia piped in, insincerely.

"Oh and one more thing. I also volunteered you for the charity auction." Sophia added at the last minute.

"What do you mean, to help with the auction?" Ashland asked hopefully, but her gut knew better.

"Oh no! I mean you'll be auctioned off for a date. Olivia and I will be participating too." Sophia informed her with a sinister grin.

"And don't worry. I'm sure some poor sucker will pay at least fifty bucks for your company." Olivia said cruelly before they both burst into a fit of giggles.

"I don't have to go, you know. I could stay home." Ashland said defiantly.

"Yes, you could. But…if you don't show, it'll look pretty bad. Especially because it's for charity. As you know, the fashion industry's elite will be in attendance. It wouldn't look good for future career opportunities, if you flake." Sophia smiled brightly, knowing she had Ashland over a barrel.

Without a word, Ashland turned and walked out the front door and walked to the elevator. Once again, she was doing everything in her power not to cry. She internally scolded herself for always turning on the waterworks when she visited her childhood home.

She had no idea what she was going to do. She had planned on wearing a simple black dress with her hair pulled back into a ponytail, to stay out of her way while she worked. It would've been the perfect ensemble to blend into the background. Now she was expected to actually attend. She didn't have a ball gown and she didn't know what to do with her hair. When it came to hair and makeup, she always stuck with the bare minimum. And not only did she not have anything to wear, but she also only had a little over an hour before the charity masquerade ball started. Which she knew was the point of her sisters' evil plan.

Ashland quickly fumbled through her camera bag for her cellphone. She called up Cisco's number and pressed send.

"Hey, Ashland! All done slaving away at Casa Del Diablo?" Cisco answered after the second ring.

"Cisco, I need your help," Ashland said, her voice filled with tears.

"What happened?" He asked immediately.

"*The Shining* twins signed me up to go to the ball as a guest and volunteered me for the charity auction. And they only just told me now. A little over an hour before the ball starts! You know I have nothing to wear!" Ashland blurted out in a panic.

"Calm down, sweetie. Meet me at the apartment. Jump in the shower and by the time you're done, I'll be there and ready to make you fabulous." Cisco assured her with confidence.

As the elevator doors opened on the main floor, several guests heading up to attend the pre-party were waiting on the other side. As Ashland quickly pushed her way through the throng of people, she collided with a very tall and very solid body. She glanced up briefly as strong hands reached out to steady her. In her rush, she saw the flash of a bright white smile, warm ocean blue eyes, and sexy blond locks. The features, vaguely familiar. Her heart stuttered in her chest, but she had no time to analyze her response. She pulled free of his large, warm hands and ran full speed for the door. Once on the street, she put her thumb and forefinger in her mouth and whistled loudly. A cab screeched to a stop in front of the building and she hopped in.

"Sullivan and Prince Street. Soho. And please hurry," Ashland said breathlessly.

~~~

Charlie Knight watched as the cab sped away. The memory of warm, plush curves against his body and in his hands, were still imprinted on his scorched palms. Satiny cocoa skin, pillowy soft lips, and large tear-filled chestnut colored eyes were seared into his brain. He didn't know who she was. He didn't know how he'd ever find her again in a city of over eight million people. Though, something in his gut told him that that moment wouldn't be the last time those lush curves would be in his arms.

Cisco lifted the back of the dress to look at Ashland's butt. She smacked at the hand that was holding up the dress.

"What are you doing?! You don't even like girls!" Ashland scolded him.

"I was looking to see if pigs were gonna fly out your ass." He smirked at her as he straightened up and dropped the fabric.

"Oh, hush! So you were able to finally get your grubby little paws on me, what's the big deal? I'll still pale in comparison to everyone else, and end up humiliated in front of all the fashion world. Especially, when no one wants to pay any money to take me on a date. I can't even get guys to take me on a date if *I* paid," Ashland said looking down at the floor.

"Look honey, maybe you want to doubt your beauty, but please don't doubt my ability to make some badass clothes. As well as my skill at making the most stubborn bud blossom into a stunning flower," he said as he clasped her shoulders. He gently turned her towards their full length mirror, she often ignored.

As Ashland took in her reflection, she was overwhelmed with emotion. Cisco had truly outdone himself. Her makeup was flawless. He had bronzed her skin into a warm, mahogany glow. Her already large eyes looked enormous from the subtle but sultry smoky eye, he had given her. Her full lips looked ridiculously inviting and plumper than usual with the shimmery plum lip gloss he had used. Her dark straight locks were swept back off of her face and neck into a sleek high bun, her bangs smoothed to one side.

Cisco had pulled her hair up to showcase her heart-shaped face, large eyes, the feminine line of her neck and the stunning mask covering half of her face. The mask was an iridescent teal blue with a few clear crystals adorning it. An intricate crystal peacock graced the right side of the mask. As elegant peacock feathers thrust out from behind it, to flutter prettily above her head with her every movement.

The whole look blended beautifully with the dress that he had designed with Ashland in mind. The ball gown was made of muted black taffeta with black crinoline peeking out the bottom, making the dress flare. Sparkling crystals embellished the dress. A few clear crystals dotted the full skirt here and there, gaining frequency as they moved up the dress. Until the bodice was completely covered in the twinkling glass. The edge of the sweetheart neckline and a band around her waist were trimmed with the glittering stone, but in the same teal blue as her mask. Knowing that she was self-conscious of her arms, Cisco gave her a sheer lace shrug with three-quarter-length sleeves. The angular cut in the back of it showing off the skin of her smooth back. Finally, the gorgeous shoes that graced her feet were three and a half inch, teal crystal covered platform heels in a comfortable size seven wide.

"Oh…Cisco! I don't know what to say!" Ashland exclaimed, staring at her image in awe.

"I'm good with 'Thank you'," Cisco teased.

Ashland have him a watery grin. "Thank you."

"Do. Not. Cry. I swear if you mess up my masterpiece, I will hurt you. Best friend or not." Cisco gave her the stink eye.

"I won't, I promise." Ashland dabbed at her eyes with her fingers, behind the mask.

"Alright…one last thing." Cisco started. "Now, this is very important. A friend of mine that works closely with a jewelry designer, let me borrow these for the night." He pulled out a black velvet box and she gasped when he opened it.

Nestled inside was a platinum necklace with a bejeweled peacock pendant. The jewels were blue topaz, aquamarine, turquoise and diamond. On either side of the necklace was a pair of platinum set, blue topaz and peridot, peacock feather design dangle earrings.

"My friend is going to stay at the design studio until twelve thirty tonight. So we have to be out of the ball by midnight, at the latest. Do you understand me? He'll have my balls in a vice, if I don't have them back." Cisco paused and then smiled. "Well, that actually wouldn't be a bad thing. He's hot! But still, I would hate for him to lose his job because of me. So don't forget." Cisco finished with a stern look.

Why does this scenario sound so strangely familiar? Nah... Ashland thought to herself.

"I won't. More than likely I'll be stuck to your side like glue the entire night." Ashland reasoned.

"True. But just in case, let's set the alarm on your phone to go off at ten 'til midnight." He grabbed her phone and pulled up the alarm to set it. "Okay, I need to go and get ready. We probably won't make it to the dinner portion of the evening, but we should at least make the auction and dance."

"That's fine. I don't think I'd be able to eat anyway. I'm too nervous to eat anything and there's really no more room left in this dress and bustier for a full stomach," Ashland said taking a deep breath and patting the tight bodice.

"How about booze? You got room for that?" Cisco smirked.

"Always!" Ashland exclaimed, blowing out a stressed breath and heading into the kitchen.

"Make me a to-go drink!" Cisco shouted out as he made his way to the bathroom.

"Coming up!"

~~~

The masquerade ball was being held at The Plaza Hotel. Ashland had been there a few times before with her father when she was younger, but the opulence never failed to amaze her. She grasped onto Cisco's arm for dear life as they made their way towards the Terrace Room. Her mouth dropped open as they walked through the French doors into the resplendent room. The design was borrowed from the essence of the Renaissance era. Grand archways, rich paintings, sculpted artwork carved into the ceiling, sparkling chandeliers and recessed lighting gave the entire room a golden glow. It all seemed incredibly romantic to Ashland. *If only my life could mirror all this*, she thought.

~~~

Little did Ashland know that her wish was soon to become true. Charlie Knight spotted her the moment she and Cisco walked through the door. As they stood on the terrace that wrapped around the room from above, the thought that came to mind was that she sparkled like a flawless diamond. Something about her radiated beauty, and looking around he could see he wasn't the only one who thought so. Many heads had turned in her direction. Even though she wore a stunning mask like everyone else at the ball. He knew that she was the dark-skinned beauty that had collided with him earlier in the evening. And he had every intention of pressing his suit before her other admirers could sink their teeth into her.

He knew the man she was with wasn't her significant other. If his bright pink tux and dramatic makeup was any indication. So with his mind made up, Charlie strode over to the stairs where they stood at the top of the landing. He watched her glance down at him and his famous smile spread naturally across his face. He noticed her ripe, delectable lips part as if she had inhaled sharply.

Charlie's long legs ate up the stairs as he made his way towards them. He stopped one step below her and still he was slightly taller than her short stature. He reached for her right hand, which looked so delicate and small in his. Charlie could tell that she was nervous, her trembling fingers and damp palm gave her away. He chivalrously bent over and softly kissed the back of her shaking hand.

Ashland nearly passed out on the spot. She squeezed Cisco's arm even harder as the sculpted lips on her skin branded her with his heat. Ashland knew who he was the moment she saw him looking up at her from the bottom of the stairs. He was Charming Charlie Knight. At least that was the nickname that had developed over the years by his adoring fans.

Charlie Knight had burst onto the modeling scene ten years ago at age eighteen. His blond godlike, boy-next-door persona endeared him to everyone. His signature smile and dimples that graced billboards across the country, had girls wanting to date him and boys wanting to be him. But three years ago, Charlie had decided to leave modeling behind to start his own magazine company, Knightly Magazine. A men's entertainment, fashion, and health magazine. Once more, his undeniable charisma launched the magazine straight to the top print and online publication. Which quickly made him one of the most eligible bachelors in the world. He was a man that knew what he wanted and stopped at nothing until it was his.

So as he looked up from her hand held tightly in his, he smiled *that* smile. All white teeth and deep dimples. His aqua blue eyes behind a silver mask, glittered brighter than the crystals on her dress. It looked as if she was the next thing he wanted. *Dear God, one could only hope. Though, wishful thinking I'm sure.*

"Hello," Charlie said.

The one word turned her knees to pudding. She knew from television interviews that he had a deep voice, but the bass in it face to face, made her panties liquefy. Ashland wasn't used to talking to men she was attracted to. So she stood there for several beats with her mouth hanging open. Cisco gave her a nudge that shook her from her stupor.

"Hi." Her voice came out in an embarrassing squeak.

"I'm Charlie Knight," he said still firmly holding onto her hand.

Ashland just blinked at him owlishly. Once again at a loss for words.

"Hi, handsome." Cisco cut in, reaching out to shake Charlie's hand. Charlie reluctantly let go of Ashland's hand to shake Cisco's. "I'm Francisco Cortez and though it would seem that my friend here is deaf and mute. I assure you she is not. She's just a little shy." Cisco turned and stared at her with bulging eyes. He looked to Ashland and then to Charlie, trying to hint to her that she should speak. "Honey, when a devastatingly handsome man introduces himself, you should reply," he whispered under his breath.

"I-I'm A-Ashland," she finally stuttered out.

"It's a pleasure to make your acquaintance, Ashland." Charlie murmured as he gladly took her hand again. "A lovely name, to go with a lovely woman. Can I get you something to drink?" Charlie asked politely as he guided her down the stairs, refusing to relinquish her hand.

Cisco quickly pried her left hand from the clutch she hand on his arm, before she dragged him down the stair. He beamed at her as Charlie led her to the bar. *Go get your man, gurl!*

Charlie pulled Ashland up to the bar and ordered her an Appletini that she quietly requested. As the bartender prepared their drinks, Charlie stared at her intently. Ashland squirmed under his heavy-lidded gaze. She had never seen a man look at her with hunger before. It was very unsettling to say the least. Once the drinks were finished, he handed Ashland her drink and finally spoke.

"So I'm one hundred percent sure that you were the beautiful woman that ran into me in the lobby of a fifth avenue building, earlier this evening. Am I right?" Charlie asked with a knowing smile.

"Oh, no! That was you?" Ashland cringed. *Way to go, Ashland! Thank God he's strong, a lesser man would've been flattened by my big ass.* She internally reprimanded herself. "I'm so sorry!" She exclaimed in humiliation.

"What do you have to be sorry about?" Charlie asked, a perplexed look wrinkled his brow. "It's not every day that a beautiful woman with soft, lovely curves crashes into me. It took all that I had not to chase after you, but I had a feeling that I'd be running into you again. And here you are." Unused to compliments from anyone except Cisco, Ashland's face heated up and she looked away bashfully.

~~~

Across the room Olivia and Sophia saw the whole scene unfold before them. They had been watching Charlie all night with an eagle eye. They had unsuccessfully tried to flirt with him at their pre-party, but he had seemed preoccupied. They also made sure that they were seated at the same table as him during the dinner portion of the evening, but again he just kept scanning the room for someone.

When his eyes had reached the top of the stairs and stayed there, they had glanced over to see what had caught his attention. They frowned in confusion when they saw a plump, dark-skinned woman in a rather lovely dress, they grudgingly admitted. They looked at each other, silently communicating, *there is no way in hell he could be interested in* that*!*

On closer inspection, as the odd couple talked at the bar, the twins realized that the girl was their frumpy stepsister.

"He couldn't possibly be interested in her!" Olivia squealed in distress. "And how did she find that ensemble in only an hour?"

"Hmm…I don't know, but he must be taking pity on her." Sophia rationalized. "Let's find out if the auction is about to start. Maybe we can speed things up a bit. I mean, he obviously needs help getting away from her and he's *way* to nice to tell her he's not interested," she suggested, clueless.

"Yes! That's perfect. He definitely needs a wingman to help him in these situations and it's apparent he doesn't have one. So we could be his wingwomen," Olivia agreed anxiously.

As the twins made their way over to talk to the organizers of the event, back at the bar, they couldn't have been more wrong. Charlie was determined to pull the shy beauty out of her shell. He wanted to know all there was to know about Ashland.

"So what do you do, Ashland?" Charlie asked, genuinely interested.

"I'm a photographer. Fashion and editorial." Ashland spoke quietly, looking down at her drink.

"Ashland, look at me," Charlie said softly as he brought his index finger to her chin to lift her face. "I know you're shy, but I want to see those beautiful brown eyes when you're saying something. I want to see what brings you passion and joy. Eyes are the windows to the soul, or so I've heard." He winked at her.

"Okay, I'll try." A small smile touched her lips.

"So what made you get into photography?" Charlie continued.

"It was my father's passion, before he built up his career and didn't have time for it anymore." Ashland shrugged. "So, I guess I decided to pick up his hobby to be closer to him after he died. And I suppose I fell in love with it like he did," Ashland said, finally getting out a whole paragraph and barely breaking eye contact. It wasn't hard considering once she looked at him, his eyes were hypnotic. Like sitting on an island beach, watching the blue waves of the ocean for hours.

"I'm sorry to hear about your dad. Though, I'm glad you found your passion. I can see how much you love it by the way your entire being lit up from the inside out," Charlie said truthfully. Unable to stop himself he raised his hand and stroked his index finger down her smooth heart-shaped face. "Are you freelance?"

"Huh?" Ashland didn't hear the question at first. She was too dazzled by his previous statement and thrown off by his gentle touch.

"Do you work freelance?" Charlie repeated.

"Oh…um…yes. I work with several different magazines and clothing stores when they need me." Ashland answered finally.

"Good. I'd love to hire you for some shoots Knightly magazine has coming up." Charlie offered.

"That would be great!" Ashland exclaimed hopefully, already anxious to see him again. "But how do you know my work is any good? Or if it would fit the layout and style of your magazine?" She asked, her insecurities once again rearing their ugly heads.

"I just do. I have a sixth sense for this kind of thing. Which has helped with my success." He took her empty glass and set it on the bar. "Would you like another-" he started before someone on a microphone cut him off.

"Alright ladies and gentlemen, our Date for the Day auction is about to begin. As soon as we get all the lovely ladies that have graciously volunteered for tonight's auction, to come up to the stage. Ladies?" The auctioneer called out.

"If you'll excuse me. One of my thoughtful stepsisters volunteered me for the auction." Ashland said with a hint of sarcasm and a tight smile.

Charlie nodded his head as she turned to walk to the stage. He smiled to himself as he realized that he'd be writing out a fat check later, because there was no way in hell he was going to let someone else win a date with Ashland.

He watched as the women lined up. Ashland was at the very end and she fidgeted nervously with her dress and clutch purse as she stood on display for the entire room. Charlie couldn't fathom why the stunning woman was so self-conscious. But he vowed that if he was lucky enough to make her his, he would make sure that she knew she was beautiful…daily.

Ashland could barely make out the people in the audience because of the bright lights that were directed towards the stage. Though she could feel eyes on her. The feeling unnerved her and her heart pounded out a beat in her ears. Her palms were a sweaty mess and she could've sworn she was on the verge of hyperventilation.

She started to take deep calming breaths as the auction began. She pretended as if she was behind her camera, the only place where she felt safe and protected. Soon, her heartbeat calmed and her breathing steadied. Once she was calm enough, she realized that the auction was well underway. And up next were her hateful stepsisters.

"Next we have the lovely, Olivia. Olivia is a runway model who enjoys walks in the park, organizing charities, and feeding the homeless at a local soup kitchen." The auctioneer listed off.

What the...? 'Feeding the homeless!' Bullshit! More like berating the homeless for being in her way! Ashland railed in her head.

"...Now the bidding will begin at one thousand dollars." The auctioneer continued.

"One thousand." Someone called out.

"One thousand to the man in the gold mask." The auctioneer verified.

"One thousand five hundred." Another voice shouted.

"Two thousand!" A man bellowed before the auctioneer could speak.

Ashland sighed deeply. *I might as well sit back and relax. This is gonna take a while.* Her stepsisters were gorgeous and Ashland knew that when it came to women's looks, men could be very superficial and fickle. It was why she still, at twenty-four-years-old had never had a boyfriend and barely been kissed. And why her stepsisters had men coming and going like a revolving door.

In the end, both stepsisters had racked up over fifty thousand dollars for charity, between the two of them. Though, Ashland did get a certain amount of pleasure when the winners of the bids for Olivia and Sophia, came up to collect their prizes. One was an old, balding pudgy man and the other was a scrawny young man, whose wire-rimmed glasses continued to slip down his nose. Her stepsisters turned up their noses, but accepted their arms reluctantly as they led them off the stage.

Now it was Ashland's turn and she took a deep fortifying breath. Even though she was trying to brace herself for humiliation, she knew that no amount of preparation would block the hurt. Though a little hopeful voice in the back of her mind told her, *Charlie still hasn't put in his bid. At least he didn't bid for Olivia or Sophia.*

Ashland glanced up in horror as she began to listen to what the auctioneer was saying. She realized too late that she didn't personally give them a list of her likes and hobbies. And considering the ridiculous lies that were said during Olivia and Sophia's introductions, she knew that they had given the organizers their lists. Which meant they had given hers as well.

"And last, but certainly not least, we have the…the bubbly and studious, Ashes." The auctioneer cleared his throat uncomfortably. Ashland wished that the floor would open up and swallow her whole. "Ashes enjoys cleaning, reading bodice-ripping romance novels on Friday and Saturday nights, and eating loads of delicious foods. For anyone wanting to take this voluptuous treat out for a day, the bidding will start at one thousand dollars."

Ashland was mortified at her introduction. What the auctioneer had said would be no big deal to someone slender and beautiful. But to a girl that was teased mercilessly by her so-called family and ignored by men, it was especially horrifying. Her stepsisters had made her look like a bookish, nerdy girl that had no life, and stuffed her face all day. With some OCD thrown in for good measure.

Even through her mask, Charlie could see the embarrassment written all over her face. He could tell that the auction was something she wasn't comfortable with, and that she had been volunteered unwillingly. Her intro wasn't as favorable as all the other women that had went before her. Charlie wondered who had written the somewhat insulting list of 'attributes'.

He gritted his teeth in anger on her behalf. Charlie had already planned on paying whatever was necessary to get that coveted date with her. Though now, he had every intention of riding up on his proverbial white horse. Wanting her pranksters to have to eat crow before the auction was over.

Before he could speak first, someone in the crowd put in their bid at a thousand dollars. Charlie scowled in the general direction of whoever had said it.

"Five thousand dollars." Charlie called out, skipping a couple thousand in the process.

"Five thousand to Charming Charlie at the bar." The auctioneer responded.

"Six thousand." A third man shouted.

"Seven thousand." The first man called back.

"Ten thousand!" Charlie growled.

The auctioneer stopped interjecting, since the men weren't letting him get in a word. His head just kept bouncing around the room as more men joined in. Many of the men had an honest interest in the shy beauty. Though, it was obvious that once Charlie had put in his bid, he had sparked interest in the other men around the room that hadn't been paying attention to her. All the men taking a second look at the curvaceous beauty standing in the spotlight. But Charlie wasn't in the mood to share. His next move squashed all the competition.

"One million," he said clear as a bell across the room. The two words shutting everyone down.

The entire ballroom grew silent as he made his way up to the stage. Ashland's wide eyes were as big as golf balls as she watched him step onto the stage. She could not believe what had just transpired. She had thought that she'd be lucky if someone even put in one bid for her. *But a million dollars! And all because of a bidding war over...ME! Unreal!*

Charlie stopped in front of her, his beautiful smile spread across his face. The bright grin warmed her like the rays of sunshine on a cool spring day. He held out his hand for Ashland to take. In the moment next that she reached across the gap between them, to place her small hand in his. Something in the universe clicked as his massive hand engulfed hers. Ashland knew that no matter what happened he'd find her, protect her, and love her. And she knew it with a certainty, she could not explain.

As Charlie walked her off the stage, Ashland saw her stepsisters and stepmother standing off to the side. They had varying expressions of disbelief written across their faces. Their mouths flapped open and closed, like a fish out of water. Ashland smiled softly and inclined her head towards them. By the looks of hatred that passed over their faces, she knew they would have ripped her apart if it wouldn't have been frowned upon.

The first strains of *What a Wonderful World* began to play from the big band. Charlie spun Ashland out, and smoothly pulled her back into the circle of his strong arms. They stayed like that for the rest of the song, swaying back and forth. She enjoyed the feel of being wrapped in his warm embrace and he relished the feel of her soft body against his. Charlie had to bite his lip hard to keep from ravishing her on the dance floor in front of everyone. Though, as the song came to an end, he looked down at Ashland and the look of naked longing on her face broke his resolve.

"Come with me," Charlie blurted out.

Clutching her hand tightly, he practically pulled Ashland from the ballroom. He led her through a set of double doors and into another ballroom, one that was currently unoccupied. He turned towards her and Ashland looked up at Charlie with a question in her eyes.

"Forgive me. I normally have more restraint than this, but never in all my life have I wanted someone as badly as I want you right now." Charlie breathed as he stepped closer to her.

Ashland's backside hit the wall and his hands rested against it on either side of her head, trapping her. He hesitated, looking down at her, asking for permission.

She gave her ascent without pause. "Please, Charlie." She whispered softly.

Charlie groaned deep in his throat before he claimed her lips as his. His hands made their way to her smooth skin. His fingers wrapped round the back of her neck, his thumbs caressed her delicate jawline as he tilted her face up further to meet his passionate kisses. His tongue flicked against Ashland's bottom lip. The shock of sensations that traveled straight to her core brought a gasp to her lips, opening her mouth to his heated assault. She had no idea where to put her hands, unused to passionate embraces. Though, she needed to do something. So her hands grasped the lapels of his tux jacket in a death grip.

Charlie growled as he aggressively stroked his tongue against hers, and Ashland responded timidly. Her sweet, little tongue that shyly touched his, nearly made him lose his mind. He at once deepened the kiss, wanting all of her, the evidence pressed painfully against his tuxedo pants.

Charlie reached up to pry one of her hands from his jacket. Slowly, he slid her open palm down his tuxedo shirt, where she could feel his defined chest and abs along the way. His body felt amazing even through his shirt. Though, she was ill-prepared for what she felt once he guided her hand to the front of his black pants.

Ashland's body shuddered and her inner walls contracted as she felt a man's hardness for the first time. Having a male roommate who adored his body, Ashland had seen male genitalia in person. Though, never hard. She didn't realize that she could be so turned on, simply by knowing she had aroused a man. She was sure that it had more to do with *this* man than anything else.

Charlie pumped forward against her hand and Ashland whimpered in response as her insides flip-flopped like a gymnast during a floor routine. He released her lips with a gasp and rested his forehead against hers. They both tried to calm their breathing.

"Ashland," Charlie said her name softly, almost desperately. "You can say no if you want, but…will you stay the night with me? I have a room here for the night, and I can't imagine anything better than burying myself inside you for the rest of the evening. No pressure, I swear. Only if you want to."

It was on the tip of her tongue to explain to Charlie that she was still a virgin or that she needed to leave by midnight, but she didn't want him to change his mind. She didn't want to wait any longer. She wanted him just as much as he wanted her and she didn't want anything to get in the way of that.

"A-Alright," she whispered hesitantly.

"Are you sure? I don't want you to think that if this doesn't happen that I won't be interested in you. Or that if it does happen that it's all I want, because the moment that you ran into me earlier, I knew I wanted you in my life…permanently," Charlie said honestly.

"I trust you." Ashland responded as she placed her hand in his.

Charlie felt overwhelmed by the gravity of the trust she was giving him. He closed his large, warm hand around hers and led her through the empty ballroom, towards the lobby elevators and pressed the call button. The doors opened immediately and Charlie pulled her in. He quickly pressed the button for the top floor, then hit the close button before anyone else could step in with them. As the doors closed, he grabbed her hips and pull her backside close against his front.

Ashland could feel his warm breath on her neck as he leaned down and hovered a few centimeters away from her anxious skin. She felt the whisper of his lips near her ear, down her neck, against her shoulder, and back up again. He breathed in deeply and then stroked his nose along the outer shell of her ear, before she felt his teeth skim the thin, sensitive skin. A shiver traveled from her hair follicles, all the way down to her toes.

"You taste just as sweet as you smell." Charlie said softly, his lips grazing her ear as he spoke.

Ashland's hands balled up into tight fists and her lips popped open when his tongue flicked the sensitive skin behind her ear. Using lips, teeth, and tongue; Charlie kissed, nibbled and licked his way down to her shoulder. His fingers scraped across her flesh as he pulled her lace shrug to the side to reveal and kiss more of the feverish skin on her shoulder. Ashland bowed back reflexively, her ass unconsciously ground into his hard bulge.

The ping of the elevator signaled their arrival on the top floor and put the sensual spell on hold. As the doors slid open, Charlie clasped Ashland's hand and led her to the door of the penthouse suite. He removed the keycard from his inside jacket pocket and opened the door. She fidgeted beside him, her nerves a frazzled mess with the anticipation of what was about to happen.

Once the door was open, Charlie only got as far as letting her in and closing the door behind them before his patience snapped. Charlie ripped his silver mask off his face, and he pushed Ashland against the door and claimed her lips once more. Without relinquishing her lush lips, Charlie quickly removed his jacket, untied his bowtie, unbuttoned his crisp white shirt and removed it as well. All the items landed on the floor at their feet.

Charlie pulled her away from the door as he began to remove her lace shrug. His lips never left Ashland's skin. He kissed her lips, jawline, and neck at the same time he backed her further into the room. His fingers found the zipper to her dress and he pulled the tab down. The dress fell to the floor in front of the massive king size bed, along with her shrug and clutch purse. Charlie stepped back to take in her plush, lovely curves.

Ashland's arm immediately came up to cover her body, left in nothing but her black lace boyshorts, matching bustier, and sparkling heels. She couldn't stand to be bare in front of Cisco when he had put the dress on her earlier, and he wasn't remotely interested in her. Standing under the gaze of a gorgeous man that appeared to want her, was sheer torture.

"Ashland, please don't cover yourself. You're stunning. These soft curves are all I've been thinking about since you ran into me." Charlie reached out and caressed the back of his index finger down her smooth cheek. "If I didn't think you were lovely, I wouldn't be about to burst out of my pants." He smirked and one dimple deepened boyishly.

Charlie gently clasped her wrists and brought them to her sides. He reached for her face and slowly removed her elaborate masquerade mask.

"That's better. Now I can see all of you…breathtaking." Charlie breathed.

Unable to hold eye contact with his intense blue gaze, Ashland's eyes traveled over him. They touched his golden hair, cut low around the sides and back and long on top. Like he was a Ken Doll come to life. His blond eyebrows, straight and long. When he wasn't smiling, like now as he stood there letting her take him in, his lips were delectably full and pink. His jawline and chin were strong as the muscle ticked there, showing his restraint. The upper part of his body was corded with muscles everywhere. It was obvious that he had stayed in shape, even after he stopped modeling. The Greek god Apollo came to mind as she looked at him. *Definitely, god of the sun…all day!*

Charlie raised his hands to the clasp and zipper on his black slacks, slowly he unfastened them. He let the pants drop to the floor and he stood before her in only his black boxer briefs. Ashland could see the outline of his erection pressed against the cotton material. She wanted to reach out and touch him, but thought better of it. Next, he grabbed the waistband of the briefs and Ashland took a deep breath. He bent at the waist as he pulled them down his legs, blocking her view. When he stood back up, Ashland expelled a huge breath as she got a full view of his naked form. Never had she imagined being with a more beautiful man.

His engorged manhood stood at attention. Proud and straight. Long and thick. Ashland's fingers twitched with the need to touch him. She timidly raised her hand and then let it drop back to her side. Charlie saw the struggle on her face and decided to coax her.

"Ashland, please. I need you to touch me," he said. His voice strained as he forced himself to hold off.

His words of encouragement and her curiosity finally brought her hand back up. Ashland reached across the few inches between them. Her fingertips lightly touched the silky smooth, yet hard mushroom tip of his impressive cock. Charlie groaned and squeezed his eyes shut at the first touch of her hands on his hot flesh. Though, not wanting to miss a moment of her discovery of his body, he quickly opened his eyes again.

Ashland's face was in deep concentration. She bit down on her bottom lip as she brought her index finger to the base of his hard length. Her finger traced a path up a thick vein, till she reached the tip and let go. Her bottom lip popped from between her teeth as she sharply inhaled, watching his cock bounce in response.

Unable to hold back any longer, Charlie's hand went to her bustier. He quickly and deftly unclasped each hook. Before Ashland could comprehend what was happening, she was on the bed. As the lacey material fell away from her skin, Charlie had twisted around and plunked her down on the bed. His fingers swiftly reached for the edge of her panties and he impatiently ripped them down her legs.

Next he was on top of her and she felt his thick manhood on her mound. Charlie's lips found hers in a deep but brief kiss. He quickly made his way down to her breasts. He swirled his tongue around her tightening areola, and she gasped and reflexively bucked against him. Ashland was a little worried that he was moving too fast, not knowing that she was a virgin. Though, everything felt so amazing, she didn't want to ruin the moment. She just hoped he'd slow down on his own.

Luckily, Charlie positioned his thick tip at her wet entrance and shallowly stroked in. In this, he wanted to take his time. He wanted to enjoy the feel of her squeezing around him, the suction of her inner walls guiding him in. Charlie made sure he held eye contact with Ashland. Her eyes widened and her hands clutched his biceps in a death grip as he stroked in a little deeper and was stopped by a barrier. *What the hell?!*

Charlie's hips went completely still and he looked down at Ashland, stunned. "Ashland, why didn't you tell me?!" He asked in utter shock and disbelief.

"I-I didn't want you to change your mind." Ashland whispered as she turned her head to the side in shame.

"That's highly doubtful." Charlie gave her a look that said she was crazy to think that he wouldn't want her either way. "This is supposed to be a special moment for you."

"It is special. Everything is perfect." Ashland defended.

"But I was treating you like someone who knew how this all worked! I should be moving slowly and getting you ready. Not ripping through your hymen like a savage beast." Charlie dropped his forehead to her chest, taking deep calming breaths as he tried to switch gears.

"Are you gonna stop? Do you not want to do this anymore?" Ashland asked with a tremble in her voice.

Charlie's head popped up and he looked down at her incredulous. "Are you kidding me?! Do you feel this?" Charlie asked as he took another shallow stroke in her tight heat. "I actually got harder the moment I realized you were a virgin. Knowing that I'll be your first and only lover is an incredible turn on. I don't think I could go back now, even if I tried." Charlie admitted.

"'First and only?'" Ashland asked skeptically, after her gasp of pleasure from the gentle strokes he was torturing her with.

"I don't think you understand that you were mine the moment you ran into me earlier. I won't…I can't let you go. So you might as well get used to this mug, because it's the only one you're gonna be looking at for the rest of your life." Charlie said emphatically.

"How romantic." Ashland teased, though she thought his words were the most romantic thing she'd ever heard.

"Mm…now stop distracting me. I have to redeem myself and do this right," Charlie said with determination.

He lowered his head and gave Ashland a soft kiss on the lips. It was sheer torture not to slam into her welcoming wetness, but Charlie knew it was his responsibility to make this just as good for Ashland. So his kisses traveled down her jaw to her neck, where he stopped to nibble and lick at the smooth skin above her erratic pulse. Her hips instinctually pumped towards him. Reluctantly, Charlie pulled all the way out of her warmth. Afraid that she'd breech her barrier before she was ready.

His travels down her body brought him to her large, chocolate tipped mounds. Charlie's hands on either side of her decadent breasts, pushed them together so that he could have easier access to both of her turgid nipples. His tongue swirled around the tips. His teeth grazed the sensitive skin. He moved his lips back and forth over them, grazing them. Taking turns with each one.

Ashland's eyes closed as she took in every sensation he was pulling from her. Her hips moved restlessly. Her back bowed off of the bed and her hands fisted in the comforter covering the bed. She thought that the feelings coursing through her couldn't get much better, but she was wrong.

Charlie sensed that she was getting close to her breaking point. He moved from her luscious breasts and made his way down her soft tummy. It wasn't tight and flat like so many women strove for, though it was soft, supple and smooth. Comforting. His.

He reached her mound at the apex of her thick thighs. She may have been a virgin, but he was surprised to find that she was well groomed. A lovely landing strip was her only adornment. He traced a finger down the strip and her hips pulled back away from him at the shock of the first touch. Charlie smirked at her futile attempt to get away from him. *She has no idea what's next.*

His lips followed the path of his finger, down the springy curls of her mound. Instead of heading straight to the tight bundle of nerves the strip pointed towards, Charlie decided to take the long way. He kissed down the crease of her inner thigh, and then slowly made his way over to her glistening labia. His lips nibbled at her nether lips. Charlie listened intently to her breathing as it hitched in her throat. He studied the movements of her body as he worked his way over it. Learning her.

Next, he made his way to her tight opening, dripping with her arousal. Charlie's tongue stroked up the middle, but he stopped before he reached her clit. He continued to taste and torment her. Her flavor was sweet and savory, and his cock felt near to bursting. He couldn't wait to get inside of her, but first he had to make sure that she came before him. Since he wasn't sure if a virgin could come internally the first time.

The agitation of her body let Charlie know that she was ready, as was he. He started from the bottom, his tongue gliding up her between her labia. He finished with a soft flick against her clit and her reaction nearly made him come on the spot. Her entire body tensed like a tightened violin string. Her upper body shot up off of the bed, her hands ripped at the comforter and sheets on the bed, and she cried out his name.

The buildup of tension in her body from his teasing assault on her, made Ashland detonate at the first flick of his tongue. Her sweet pussy flooded with her honeyed nectar and Charlie lapped it up eagerly, as her cries reached his ears. Eventually, Ashland was unable to take much more and she pushed at his head, signaling for him to stop. Charlie crawled back up her lush body and positioned his near erupting cock at her entrance.

He gazed into her eyes for a few beats, asking for permission. Ashland looked up at him with heavy-lidded eyes and nodded her head. With swift precision, Charlie plunged into her welcoming tightness and through the delicate barrier. Her eyes widened and her back arched as the pain hit her and he groaned at the feel of her still fluttering walls around him.

Buried to the hilt, Charlie stilled as he waited for her to get accustomed to his size.

"Are you okay?" He asked breathlessly.

"Mmhmm." Ashland hummed and nodded her head, not trusting herself to speak.

Testing the waters, she pumped up towards him. Instead of the pain she thought she'd feel, ripples of pleasure washed over her. She inhaled sharply at the feeling. Charlie took that as his queue to continue. Placing his hands on either side of her head, he slid out to the tip, and plunged back in. He hit the top of her cervix and a scream tore from her throat.

"Ahh God!" Charlie shouted out. "I can't take much more. Are you ready?"

"Yes, please!" Ashland answered. Though, she didn't really know what he was asking but she quickly found out.

Charlie grasped her hips with strong sure hands. Once more he pulled out to the head of his staff, but this time when he thrust forward he didn't stop. He pounded into her pliant flesh over and over again. Ashland's hands found his forearms as she tried to hold on for dear life. With every inward stroke, her cries became louder and louder.

Charlie's body glistened with sweat. His blond hair flopped on his forehead with his aggressive movements. His teeth clenched together as he growled deeply with every pump of his hips. He was mindless to everything but the connection of their most intimate place. He felt the beginnings of her impending climax as her walls contracted around him. He slowed his speed by a fraction and added a swivel to his hips and it was game over.

Ashland's nails dug crescent shaped indents into Charlie's forearms as her orgasm ripped through her. Her body convulsed uncontrollably around him, pulling an explosive climax from him as well. Charlie quickly pulled out and his seed pumped from his body onto her trembling belly. Charlie leaned forward, rested his forehead against hers and softly kissed her nose.

"Was that okay?" Charlie asked in concern.

"Lord, yes! That was incredible." Ashland sighed.

"But I didn't hurt you, did I? Cause I mean, I did get a little carried away." Charlie said with a shy boyish look on his face.

"It hurt at first, but it felt really good after that." Ashland assured him just as shyly.

"Good." He grinned happily, before kissing her forehead and getting up from the bed. "Let me get a towel to clean you up."

"Okay." She looked away bashfully as she saw the evidence of her virginity on his semi hard length.

Charlie strode into the massive bathroom. He grabbed a washcloth and wet it under the faucet. He quickly wiped away the blood and cum from his body. He wet two more towels and walked back into the room.

Ashland hadn't moved a muscle as she waited for him. Her mahogany skin had a radiant afterglow that only came from good sex. She smiled self-consciously as he strode towards her. The vision of her lying there with his seed on her dark chocolate body, made the blood resurge to his cock. Her eyes widened in surprise as she watched his nearly flaccid member swell up and out once more.

Charlie tried to ignore his body's reaction to her. Instead he concentrated on cleaning her up. He grabbed her around the back of her thighs and pulled her butt to the edge of the bed. He quickly wiped away the remnants of their lovemaking. One towel wiped away the mess he had left on her stomach and the other, he very gently wiped at the tender flesh between her legs. The sweet gesture brought tears to her eyes. It had been a long time since she had been treated with anything remotely close to love and affection.

He finished with his gentle ministrations and tossed the towels on the floor. Charlie looked down at her and saw the tears glistening in Ashland's eyes. He quickly leaned forward and began to kiss her, all over her face. The tears that had been trembling on her lids, spilled over and he kissed the tracks that they made down her temples.

"Why are you crying?" Charlie asked with concern.

"I'm happy." Ashland choked out.

His freshly hardened erection was poised at her entrance as he brushed the tears away from her face. Being in such a convenient position, Charlie slid into her awaiting core once more. He continued to plant sweet kisses all over her face, while he gently pumped his hips forward. Her restless body again told him that she wanted more. He stood up and placed her abundant, shapely legs on his chest and stomach and thrust home. The angle brought him in deeper than before and they both threw back their heads at the deep penetration.

Charlie's talented hips brought them both to a stunning climax. He used what little energy he had left to clean her off again with one of the towels he had tossed to the side.

He then collapsed next to her and they both instantly drifted off to sleep in each other's arms.

~~~

Ashland's alarm on her cellphone jarred her awake. *Shit!* She quickly slid out of the circle of Charlie's arms. She didn't think of much other than not wanting to piss off Cisco or get his special friend in trouble. She threw her dress over her naked body and fought with the zipper, only getting it to the middle of her back. So to cover the gaping material, she grabbed Charlie's white dress shirt and put it on and tied the ends around her waist. She quickly reached down and snatched up her panties, bustier, clutch purse and shoes. She scrambled to the door and out the penthouse suite barefoot. She ran over to the elevator and pressed the down button. She'd worry about putting on her shoes and straightening her clothes when she got in the elevator.

The elevator finally arrived and Ashland jumped in and hit the button for the main level. She quickly shoved her panties into her tiny purse. She went to put on her shoes and realized that she only had one. *Dammit!* She knew she didn't have time to go back up to find it. It wasn't ideal to run around the streets of New York City barefoot, but she'd rather do that than face the wrath of her roommate.

The elevators pinged its arrival on the bottom level. When the doors opened, miraculously, Cisco was standing there.

"Oh, thank God! I was about to knock on every damn door on every floor to find you. I've been looking everywhere for you." Cisco said as he pulled Ashland towards the doors of the fancy hotel. "Where have you been?" He asked, finally stopping to actually get a good look at her and his brown eyes widened as he took in her disheveled appearance and Charlie's shirt. "Oh. OH! Holy shit! He popped your-"

"Stop!" Ashland held up her hand as they jumped into a cab.

Cisco quickly gave the cabbie the cross streets to their destination before turning back to his best friend.

"So you're not going to give me any details. I mean, that was Charming-fucking Charlie for fuck's sake! You have to tell me *something*!" Cisco whined.

"It was amazing. Superb. Life-changing! Is that good enough?" Ashland asked in frustration.

"Barely." Cisco pouted. "Was it big?" He pressed on.

Ashland gave him an exasperated look before answering. "Yes. Now that's enough."

"You're no fun." Cisco scrunched up his face, petulantly. "Well are you at least going to see him again?"

Ashland gasped in horror. "Oh no!!!! He was asleep when I left and I didn't leave my number or anything. He doesn't even know my last name!" She cried out in devastation.

"Don't even worry about it, honey. He's one of the richest men in the city. He'll be able to find you. Especially since you're in the same industry. Besides, you could always go to him. I mean, seriously. You know he owns a magazine. You could always try to get in through your photography." Cisco suggested.

"I know. I just wouldn't feel right. I'd feel desperate." Ashland said sadly, hoping that he would find her.

"It's up to you, sweetie. But I have a feeling it'll all work out." Cisco patted her hand.

"I hope so."

Charlie slowly awoke from an amazing dream about Ashland. A sleepy smile spread across his face as he stretched and reached out for her. When his hand connected with thin air and cold sheets, his eyes flew open and he sat up quickly. She was nowhere to be seen. He realized that her clothes were missing and that she must have left at some point in the middle of the night. Charlie's stomach dropped. He jumped out of the bed and checked the entire suite. When he found no sign of her, for some reason unknown to him, he strode over to the door and opened it. As if she'd be standing on the other side. His eyes instantly fell upon the evidence of her quick departure. Lying there on its side was one of her crystal heels.

Charlie propped open the door so it would lock him out and he walked over to the little sparkling shoe. *Why would she leave without saying anything? Did I do something to upset her? How am I going to find her?* He thought frantically as he picked up the beautiful footwear.

Logic stopped him before he began to panic. *Stop Charlie, think. You know she's a photographer for several magazines. How many Ashland's could there be that works as a freelance photographer for fashion magazines?*

Charlie walked back into the room and found his pants on the floor. He searched his pockets for his cellphone. He pulled up his contacts list and started making some phone calls.

~~~

Ashland made her way around the racks of clothing, makeup and hair stations, as well as people and models in different states of dress. She gave the models who were half dressed some privacy, but other than that she took pictures of everything. She wanted to document everything for Cisco's big moment. New York fashion week was a big deal and she had no doubt that he'd be invited to participate in Paris, London, and Milan too.

After taking several shots of the chaos behind the scenes, she made her way to the front where seats were filling up fast. She snapped shots of the audience and empty runway. She setup shop at the end of the runway before the show started and kicked off her knee high boots. As always preferring to work barefoot.

When the show began. she got shots of each model as they came to the end of the long runway. The plus size models looked stunning in Cisco's creative and flattering styles. The audience ohhed and ahhed over his creations and at the end when he came out at the tail end of the model procession. The audience gave him a standing ovation and cheered enthusiastically. Ashland wanted to clap like a maniac too, but she needed to make sure she didn't miss one single shot for him.

She became distracted from her friend's special moment as he began his speech to end the show, when she felt someone behind her. Ashland turned around and saw her stepsisters and mother standing there with murderous looks on their faces. It was obvious they had just come from modeling in another runway show, if the dramatic makeup on their faces was any indication.

"You think you got your grubby little, fat hands on Charlie, but there's no way that he'd be more interested in you than either of us. He'll realize that you're a fat slut and lose interest. So you better watch your back step*sister* because we will ruin you and your career." Sophia sneered at her.

A knot of emotions formed in Ashland's throat, her insecurities feeding off the thought that they were probably right. Charlie probably would forget about her. Before she could respond though, she heard Cisco call out her name over the microphone.

"And I just want to thank my best friend in the whole world for inspiring this entire collection. Ashland come on up here." Cisco called out to her.

She was not even close to being prepared to go up on stage in front of a room full of her peers. Especially not, since she was about to burst into tears from her sisters' cruelty and she was completely barefoot. Ashland hesitated, but Cisco wasn't taking no for an answer. So she self-consciously made her way up to the raised runway. Cisco helped her up and as the cheers increased, for lack of anything better to do, Ashland did a little curtsy and ducked her head prettily.

The crowd started to quiet down and their eyes followed movement coming towards them. Ashland looked to where they were staring and saw a tall figure making its way over. The lights above the runway blinded her for a moment and then standing below her was her knight. Charlie. His signature grin was spread across his face. His dimples nearly made her knees buckle.

Charlie looked up at her with his hands behind his back. The phone calls he had made earlier in the day had finally lead him here. Seeing her again was like a balm to his frazzled nerves. She was adorable in formfitting skinny jeans, a long shapeless sweater that hung off one shoulder, a colorful scarf around her neck, and cute bare feet. Her hair was pulled back into a schoolgirl ponytail. Her bangs were down with wispy tendrils on either side.

"I missed you this morning." Charlie said quietly.

"I'm so sorry. I didn't mean to leave so abruptly. I had to leave before midnight to return the jewelry I was wearing." Ashland whispered, completely aware that the room at large was listening to their conversation.

"Well, I had to find you. You left something behind in your rush. And I wanted to give it to you." Charlie said as he brought the sparkling blue shoe around to show her.

"Is that the only reason you had to find me?" Ashland asked softly.

"Well, it might seem a little soon, but I also wanted to ask what you were doing the rest of your life?" Charlie asked his face completely serious.

"S-Spending it with you?" Ashland posed it as a question. Her voice was wobbly with tears.

"If you'll have me?" Charlie responded honestly, holding out the shoe for her.

"Abso-freakin'-lutely!" She blurted out as she slid her foot into the shoe.

Before he knew what hit him, Ashland launched herself into Charlie's strong arms. His reflexes were quick and he caught her perfectly. The crowd burst into applause around them. Startling them, considering they had forgotten they weren't alone. Her stepmonster and evil stepsisters stormed out of the building in an angry huff.

Cisco grinned knowingly. The hint of a sparkle twinkled in his eye. *I'm the best fucking fairy godmother ever!*

~~~

With the help of Charlie and his lawyer, a few short months later, Ashland found out that her father's magazine, La-La Land, was actually willed to her. Her stepmother was only supposed to take over until Ashland was legally old enough to run the company. The penthouse apartment was also hers as well. Ester was only allotted one million dollars for the one year, she and Ashland's father were married, before his death. And since she had already ran through that money long ago, she really had no rights over anything. Which was why she used her domineering nature to manipulate Ashland into believing she owned nothing.

So with no other recourse, she and her daughters moved to one of the outer boroughs of New York and her stepsisters' careers quickly became fledgling once they didn't have the company to back them. Including the fact that the industry was fed up with their diva behavior. Eventually, they were reduced to modeling in catalogs.

Ashland quickly took back her cherished childhood home and rebuilt her father's magazine. Restoring its class and stellar reputation. She and Charlie married a year later. Combining both their empires. She didn't have much time for her favorite hobby anymore, but every now and again when the urge hit her, she had the perfect model at home and in her bed. With Charlie's praise and learning the ropes of running a company, Ashland no longer needed to hide behind the camera lens. And she realized that though her life wasn't perfect, she had found her own little slice of happily ever after.

••••

Bonita

Rocco Bennett stepped out the front door of his lavish loft apartment building. The light of the full moon illuminated the sidewalk as he took off down his street towards the park, on his nightly jog. As he ran along the concrete path, he came towards a stunning, tall and slender brunette as she walked to her car parked along the street. Her arms were filled with bags as she fumbled with her car keys. She clumsily dropped them and they fell down off the curb and under her car. Roc quickly ran over to assist the gorgeous woman.

"I've got it." Roc said as his white smile spread across his handsome, dark mahogany face.

"Oh, thank you." The woman replied sweetly.

Roc got down on his hands and knees to search for her keys. Unable to see, he pulled his phone out of his shorts' pocket and turned on its flashlight. Finding the keys, he grabbed them and then hopped back up onto his feet. Roc handed the young woman the keys, letting his fingers linger on her soft skin.

"I really appreciate the help. That was so sweet of you." The brunette looked up at him from under her eyelashes. "I'm Denise," she said adjusting her bags to shake his hand.

"I'm Roc. Here let me help you with those bags." He suggested gallantly.

Roc took her heavy bags as she opened her car door. After she was done transferring the bags from his arms to her backseat, Denise boldly asked for Roc's cellphone. Once he handed it to her, she then proceeded to add her name and number to his contacts. When she was finished, Roc said his goodbyes and grinned arrogantly as he started back down the street.

He had only made it a few feet when he saw a cute, plump blonde struggling with a jack to lift her car to fix a flat tire. She glanced up as she heard Roc coming towards her. She smiled brightly, hopeful.

Roc took in her plump body and quickly turned up his nose. He kept his eyes straight ahead, callously ignoring the woman. She still didn't give up hope that he'd stop to assist her and as he came closer, she spoke.

"Excuse me? Do you think you could help me really quick?" She asked sweetly.

"Sorry." Roc responded as he kept going.

"Wow, really? Are you sure about that?" She asked again, almost as a warning.

Roc continued on, not giving the woman a second thought and picked up his pace. He missed the low growl that emanated from the woman's throat as her eyes morphed into the gold color of an animal. *You will finally learn Rocco Bennett...*

~~~

Bo was walking through the dark library parking lot to her car when a massive arm, like a steel band wrapped around her body and yanked her off her feet. The other hand quickly clamped down over her mouth before the scream that was trapped in her throat, could signal her distress. Her legs kicked wildly, but her efforts were futile against the strength of her attacker.

An incredibly deep and gravelly, baritone voice whispered in her ear. "If you don't stop fighting, I'll be forced to knock you out." Her attacker growled.

All Bo could think about was the well-known warning to never let an attacker get you in a car because once he gets you there, you're dead. So his words only made her fight harder. A few seconds later the hand over her mouth moved and a raw scream ripped from her throat, but it didn't last long. The hand came back over her lips and nose, but this time holding a sweet smelling cloth over her face. *NO!* Her heart nearly exploded in panic as her world went black.

~~~

Roc sighed heavily, he didn't want to knock out the beautiful voluptuous Latina, but it was a means to an end. *I have no choice.* He lifted her effortlessly and placed her limp body in the back of his SUV. He quickly tied her wrists and ankles together, and placed duct tape across her plump, shapely lips. He didn't want the normally quiet librarian to wake up and cry for help or escape.

Roc desperately needed the plan he'd devised to work. If not, his dark secret would eventually consume him. Every month, at the time of the full moon, he'd lose consciousness only to wake up in the morning naked and covered in blood. He had no idea what or who he had killed, but he knew it wouldn't be long before he'd be caught if he was killing humans. He didn't want to believe that he was a monster. A werewolf. In fact, he even refused to say the word out loud.

He had searched around for years trying to find anyone that could help him. Which was when he stumbled across GenLabs, several months ago. A laboratory that focused on the study of genetics. Doctor Miguel Cabrera was a brilliant genetics scientist that Roc knew could help him find the key to end his curse. Though the man refused to see Roc, always saying that he didn't have time to see patients, and to go see a regular physician.

So with no other choice, Roc decided to force the man's hand. By kidnapping and holding his daughter, Bonita Cabrera hostage until he could find the cure. Roc had been watching her and her father for months. The thirty-year-old still lived with her father in San Francisco and though she was smart enough to have been a doctor like her father. Bo chose to live her life with her nose in a book and as the head librarian of the city's public library.

All of Roc's researching and staking out the two had led him to this moment. He knew Miguel doted on his daughter and would do anything for her. Roc was depending on it. So after he was finished securing the woman, he took out his phone and snapped a picture of her bound and unconscious body as leverage.

He closed the back door and jumped in the driver's seat. He drove up the dark winding road to his sprawling home deep in the Northern California Mountains. Roc had amassed a fortune from the internet company he started and had become an arrogant socialite. Though, a late night jog five years ago was when everything changed.

Roc had went out for a jog that evening, like he always did. Whenever he needed to think, a hard run would always help. Plus, it kept him in shape and he was nothing, if not meticulous about his physical appearance.

The run had started out like normal, outside of his renovated loft apartment. He had made his way to one of the parks he liked to run through, after stopping to help a damsel in distress. As he ran, he felt like someone was watching him. Before he knew what was happening, someone or some*thing* had attacked him. In the few seconds that the attack took place, Roc was unable to make out what it was. All he knew was that he was left for dead in the middle of the park.

He had been taken to the hospital and made a full recovery. Although, he was left with three claw marks marring his handsome face. It wasn't until a month later that the first blackout happened, and happened every month thereafter. When he realized what was going on, he sold his cherished loft apartment and bought a home in the mountains. Roc became a virtual hermit, conducting his business from within his fortress. The guilt, shame, and fear of hurting someone kept him away from the human population for the last five years.

Roc pulled up to the gate of his home and punched in the code. He parked alongside his front door and went to the back of his vehicle. He lifted Bo into his arms and carried her into his home, towards the east wing of his massive estate. He carried her limp body to the room he had prepared for her. The windows were barred so she couldn't escape. Roc laid her on the huge king size bed, unbound her wrists and ankles, and pulled the tape from her mouth.

He looked down at her peaceful form and knew he'd have a battle on his hands when she woke up. But first things first, he had an unscheduled meeting with her father. So leaving her on the bed, Roc backed out of the room and closed the door. He locked and barred it to insure that she was going nowhere.

~~~

"I'm here to see Dr. Cabrera." Roc said to the guard at the front desk of the lab.

"Do you have an appointment or meeting scheduled with Dr. Cabrera?" The bored guard asked, flipping through the day's paper.

"No, I don't." Roc said already wanting to bash the man's head in, knowing he was about to give him a hard time.

"Then, I'm sorry. Dr. Cabrera isn't meeting with anyone that doesn't have an appointment." The guard said, glancing up from his newspaper.

"You might want to tell him that it's urgent and in regards to his daughter. She may be in danger." Roc ground out through clenched teeth.

The guard sighed heavily and put down the newspaper. "Fine. I'll take you to him."

Roc followed the guard down the white sterile halls of the lab. The florescent lights overhead bounced off of the white floors, walls, and ceiling nearly giving him a migraine. Especially, considering he only existed in his dark depressing house for the past five years.

Finally, after walking down the endless maze of nondescript halls, the guard stopped in front a door. He opened it and gestured inside.

"Here ya go," he said before walking away.

Wow. Way to guard the employees. I could be some psycho mass shooter. Or some crazy person that just kidnaped the doctor's daughter. Roc shook his head as he watched the guard saunter off. He turned and stepped into the room. An older Hispanic gentlemen with a full head of salt and pepper hair was bent over a microscope. *Put on your game face.*

"Dr. Cabrera?" Roc spoke, startling the other man.

Miguel Cabrera looked up to see a massive dark-skinned black man standing in the entrance of his personal office. A quick analysis in the doctor's head estimated that the man hovering in the doorway was around six-foot-five and about two-hundred and sixty pounds of solid muscle. A genetic masterpiece. *Aside from the three angry scars running down the right side of his face,* Miguel thought.

"Yes, I'm Dr. Cabrera. Can I help you?" Miguel asked. Normally he would have shouted at anyone who would dare disturb him, but looking at the mountain of a man had him rethinking his approach.

"I need your help." The man's deep voice vibrated throughout the room as he stepped further inside and shut the door. Miguel instantly got nervous.

"With what exactly?" Miguel asked curiously.

"I…I have a condition and I've been searching for a cure. So I figured, who better to talk to than an expert in genetics." Roc explained.

"I'm sorry, sir. But I just don't have time to take on anything else at the moment." Miguel said firmly.

"I was afraid you'd say that." Roc pulled out his phone and pulled up the pic of a bound and gagged Bo. "I'm not asking you. I'm telling you to help me." He slid the phone across the doctor's desk. The phone hit the base of the microscope, stopping. And the doctor looked down at the screen. The instant he saw his daughter, he looked up in horror at the large man towering over him. "She's safe…for now." He responded to the fear in the older man's eyes.

"Where is she?" Miguel burst out, ready to do battle, though he knew he'd lose.

"I think you know that telling you her location would defeat the purpose." Roc raised an eyebrow. "But she will be staying with me until you can help cure me of this…this curse. Though, the quicker the better for your daughter's safety."

"What's wrong with you?" Miguel asked angrily.

"I know you won't believe this, but I think it's best for your daughter if you take me seriously." Roc prefaced before taking a deep breath and plunging ahead. "Five years ago, I was attacked by something. I was left for dead, but recovered. A month later, on the night of a full moon, I blacked out. When I came to, I was naked and covered in blood. This strange occurrence has happened every month, every full moon since. I have no idea what or who I hurt each time, but I have no intentions of living the rest of my life like this. So we have one month to figure out the cure before it happens again with your daughter in my possession." Roc finished with a warning.

"So you're telling me that you think you've turned into what? A werewolf?" Miguel asked incredulous.

"That's exactly what I'm telling you." Roc placed his hands on Miguel's desk and leaned forward till they were practically nose to nose. "It's your choice if you want to think I'm crazy, but what if I'm not? Do you really want your daughter under my care a month from now?"

Miguel swallowed audibly. "No," he whispered.

"Good." Roc shoved off of the desk. "And don't even think about telling the police. Just keep remembering that your daughter will be safe as long as you keep your mouth shut and you help me." Roc threatened.

"Fine. But so help me God, if you harm a hair on her head, once I cure you, I'll kill you myself." Miguel said bravely.

"Agreed." Roc held out his hand.

Miguel grudgingly took the offered hand and shook it.

"Well, I might as well get started now, if I want my daughter back. Have a seat and I'll take some of your blood and cotton swab your mouth for DNA to analyze." Miguel sighed and pulled up his sleeves. Ready to go to work to save his daughter.

~~~

Bo slowly drifted up into consciousness. She felt groggy as she cracked opened her eyes and her head pounded brutally. The room she was in was dark, but her eyes quickly adjusted. She took in the large room while she tried to remember what happened. *Where am I?*

A sudden flash of memory hit her and her hands clamped over mouth as a cry burst from her lips. Bo remembered strong arms lifting her off of her feet in the library parking lot. She recalled the deep gravelly voice of her kidnaper before the sickly sweet smell of chloroform against her face.

    She fearfully scanned the room one more time and once she realized that she was alone, she jumped off of the bed and ran to the window. It was still dark out and she wondered if it was still the same night. Looking out the window all she could see was the pale moonlight against the shadows of tall trees. Beyond that, she had no idea where she was.

    Bo opened the window and tested the iron bars. They didn't budge in the slightest. She quickly ran to the door and tested the knob, but it didn't move either. Frantic, she ran to every door to find a way out. She looked in the attached bathroom and the empty walk-in closet, but there was absolutely nothing.

    She had no idea what was going on or who had taken her. She felt the panic rising up to choke her. Still in the closet, Bo slid down the wall. She wrapped her arms around her torso as if she was trying to hold herself together. Her head fell back against the wall as hot tears slipped down her face in a torrent of helpless fear.

~~~

    Roc came home a few hours later, with his heart filled with hope and a suitcase filled with clothes for Bo. Her father had insisted that he bring her a change of clothes. Roc made his way upstairs to her designated room. He took a deep breath before unlocking the door, unsure of how the next few minutes were going to go.

    He quickly scanned the room as he walked inside, when he didn't see Bo in the bed where he'd left her. Roc turned on the bedroom light, placed her suitcase on the empty bed and strode into the bathroom, but she wasn't there either. *She couldn't have possibly gotten out!* He walked over to the closet and opened the door there. He almost missed her and closed the door, but he looked down briefly and saw her curled up tightly on the floor, trying her best not to be seen.

Roc flipped on the light in the closet and his dark eyes connected with hers. Her eyes were a beautiful light brown shade that sparkled with tears that trembled on her lids. He took a step closer into the closet, wanting to comfort her and she cringed away in fear. Roc stopped in his tracks, realizing that she didn't know him the way he knew her, from months of watching from a distance. She had no idea if he'd hurt her or not and he was certain that the scary jagged scars down his face didn't help. Everyone seemed scared of him now.

"I won't hurt you," Roc said deeply.

Bo looked up at him skeptically.

"I brought some of your clothes for you, if you need to change." He informed her.

"H-How? Did…did you hurt my father?" Bo asked.

"No. Your father packed the clothes himself." At Bo's shocked expression, Roc explained further. "Your father is helping me and in return, when he's finished I will release you to him. Until then, you'll be in my care. I won't hurt you, but please don't try to escape because it's not possible. Even if you got outside of the house and gate around the perimeter of my estate, we're up in the mountains. You'd die out in the wilderness before you could ever reach help." Roc warned her.

"If my father knows I'm here, he'll call for help." Bo's voice trembled as she tried to put up a brave front.

"Your father knows I have you, but no idea where. Besides, he wouldn't take a chance at alerting the police, when I warned him that you'd be in jeopardy if he did. So you see, there's no getting out of this. You're here to stay for the time being. So get used to it." Roc said firmly, brooking no argument.

"Screw you!" Bo screamed at him as tears streamed down her face. "You can't fucking keep me here! It's just not right." Roc turned to leave the closet as she continued to yell, but her next words stopped him. "You're a monster!"

Roc's back was still turned to her, when his shoulders slumped slightly. "You have no idea." He whispered and then walked out of the closet and bedroom, and bolted the door.

Bo rocked back and forth as heart-wrenching sobs ripped from her chest. Her life had been a series of mundane routines. Nothing exciting ever happened to her. So she lived out her fantasies within the books she read, to the point that she made books her job. Being a librarian, she was surrounded by her one true love every day. Though, when she prayed for a fraction of the adventure the heroes and heroines in her books experienced, she never asked for this.

~~~

Roc punched a hole through one of the walls of his master bedroom. He felt nothing and when he pulled his hand out from the damaged drywall, there wasn't a scratch to be seen. One advantage of the curse was even when he was in his human form; he was faster, stronger, and more agile. Though, he'd give anything to have his life go back to the way it once was. *Well, almost...*

Before the attack, before the claw marks running down his face, Roc was an arrogant man. He knew he was handsome and physically fit, and he made sure he did all of the things to keep up his physical appearance. He could walk into any room and turn the heads of women and men alike. The ladies sought him out and he had the pick of the litter. And he was a man's man. Most men wanted to be around him, to be buddies.

When it came to the ladies, Roc would only pick the most beautiful with bodies to match. He knew he had been a superficial asshole, but he didn't care at the time. Someone like Bo would've never appealed to him. He would've thought of her as one of the chubby girls. The tagalong friend of the beautiful girl. Though in his self-imposed banishment, his view of the world and people started to shift.

None of the girls that he had dated previously would have stood by his side during this curse and his subsequent exile. In fact, while he was recovering in the hospital, no one came to see him. He quickly realized that all of his relationships were superficial. No one truly cared about him as a person. As a human being.

After the attack; his massive muscular physique, tall stature, and angry scars running down the right side of his face. Not to mention the predatory vibe that oozed from him. Made him look scary as hell. Strangers took a wide berth when crossing his path and the people he knew couldn't look him directly in the eye anymore. That was when he ran to the mountains to hide away from everyone and everything.

When he started watching Bo and her father several months ago, he saw the caring in the plump woman's eyes. The way she took care of her father. How she would patiently help anyone that came into the library. Roc had even seen her give her lunch to a homeless man that was sitting outside of the library, taking shelter from the rain.

The memories of her kindness was what made her calling him a monster that much harder. *If this woman that can see the good in anyone, can't see it in me, I must not be worth shit.* What killed him the most was that before the unwelcome curse, he actually was a monster on the inside. In his solitude, he learned a lot about himself and what mattered most. Roc felt that now, he was a better person for it on the inside, but on the outside he now looked like the monster he once embodied. Basically, his life had turned into a cruel joke that he knew he deserved and had brought on himself.

If he was honest with himself, he would admit that during the months he stalked Bonita Cabrera, he had fallen in love with the curvaceous woman. The kindness, intelligence and honesty he had witnessed in her made her inner beauty shine. And during that time he saw the appeal in her physical appearance as well.

Her long chestnut brown hair swayed hypnotically at her tailbone as she walked. Her narrow waist above the breadth of her wide hips as she walked, was seductive. The softness of her tummy and thighs made Roc want to pull her close to snuggle up and never let go. Her small, pert breasts would fit perfectly in his mouth and hands. He felt he could get lost in her bright amber colored eyes. And he was desperate to taste her plump, pouty lips.

Roc sighed deeply, as he stared at the fresh hole in the wall he now had to fix. He knew the likelihood of Bo ever letting him get close to her was slim to none. He walked over to his dresser, quickly stripped off his jeans and t-shirt and grabbed a pair of gray sweats to throw on for the night.

He knew Bo had to be hungry, since he snatched her up before she could get home to fix dinner. So Roc made his way to his chef's kitchen and reheated the soup he had prepared for her arrival. Cooking was something that he enjoyed. It helped to calm his nerves when running couldn't. Earlier he had made homemade tomato soup for his guest and now he started on making her a gourmet grilled cheese to go with it.

Once her food was ready; Roc placed the bowl of soup, sandwich, and a glass of water on a tray to take up to her room. He left his plate and bowl in the kitchen to eat after he delivered Bo her tray of food. Roc would've liked nothing more than to eat with her, but he figured he'd be pushing his luck.

Balancing the tray with ease, Roc made his way upstairs and down the hall. He took a deep breath and knocked on Bo's door. He listened closely but there was no sound coming from the other side.

"Bo? I brought you some dinner," Roc said listening closely for a response. He still heard nothing. "I hope you're decent because I'm coming in." He warned.

Roc unbolted and unlocked the door and opened it slowly. Bo sat on the bed, puffy-eyed and silent. Her long hair shielded half of her face from his view. Roc looked away guiltily.

"I made some soup and a sandwich for you." Roc said quietly, his deep voice rumbling in his chest.

"I'm not hungry." Bo said tight-lipped.

"Well, you will be at some point." Roc said logically.

"I'd rather starve to death than eat anything you bring me." Bo growled.

"Bo, don't be a child. You have to eat." Roc said trying to hold on to his patience.

"Don't speak to me like you know me. You know nothing about me!" Bo shouted out boldly.

Roc's jaw flexed as he gritted his teeth in frustration. He practically slammed her tray on the nightstand next to the bed. The soup slopped over the side of the bowl. He placed his balled up fists on the soft mattress and leaned close to her.

"I know just about everything that there is to know about you. I watched you for months before I took you." Bo's head snapped around to look at him in shock. "Yeah, that's right. I know that you're dad has taken care of you since you were little, after your mother died in a car accident. I know that you love books more than you like people, but the people you do know, you treat with kindness and respect. And when someone is in pain, you feel it in the depths of your soul.

"I know that you cook for your father every night and that you love to read in the park on Sundays, if the weather is nice." Roc slowly stood up and Bo's eyes followed him. "I know that you've had only one boyfriend and that he cheated on you. Funny enough, you didn't cry or care when you found out. In fact, you were relieved when you broke up with him two years ago. You haven't even attempted to date since. Instead, when you get lonely, you pick up a classic romance to fill the void. Does that all sound about right?" Roc finally finished.

Bo quickly turned her head away from Roc's probing gaze. She held her chin up high as she tried to ignore him.

"That's what I thought." Roc started to turn to head back out of her room, but he stopped to add one more thing. "If you were mine, I'd never cheat and you'd never have to crack open a romance novel again. You'd never have to seek out satisfaction from a fictional hero, if I had anything to say about it." Roc informed her before he walked out of her room and locked the door.

Bo stared at the closed door in astonishment. Never had anyone, let alone a man, read her so well before. It was disconcerting to have someone get to the very heart of her without her knowledge of it happening. But what bothered her the most was that she wasn't as bothered as she should've been, by the fact he had apparently stalked her. *What the hell is wrong with you, Bo?! You should be totally freaked out right now. Big arms, ripped abs, and a killer face should not be good excuses to ignore psychotic behavior.*

When Roc had walked into her room with her dinner, Bo hadn't expected him to be in just a pair of sweats and nothing else. She had tried to ignore his silky, smooth dark chocolate skin and the muscles rippling underneath the surface. His shiny bald head gleamed in the light of the glittering chandelier overhead. His jet black goatee was groomed to perfection, emphasizing crazy full lips. Bo was sure that Roc was the most gorgeous man she had ever seen, even with the angry scars running down the right side of his face. They only succeeded in adding a level of danger to his handsome face.

I have to get out of here before I do something stupid. Like fall in love with my psycho captor. They do say that one of the stages in abduction is being grateful to your captor for taking care of you. Fuck that noise! Who's they anyway? More than likely someone who's never been abducted.

Bo's stomach growled and she reluctantly accepted the fact that she was starving. She scooted back until her back rested against the headboard and then she placed the tray of food on her lap. She hesitantly brought the first spoonful of soup up to her lips and took a tentative sip. Bo closed her eyes, savoring the flavor. She then dropped her head down in exasperation at how wonderful the food was that he had made. *Oh, it would be delicious! Ugh...*

She tucked into her food as she began to formulate a plan of escape.

~~~

Bo had to wait a week before the first opportunity arose to make her getaway. It had been a week of pure torture. Roc was kind and warm towards her. He brought her delicious food three times a day. All homemade and all apparently cooked by him. Bo was sure that he was trying to win her over through her stomach.

She tried her best to remain aloof. She made little to no conversation when he would visit her. It killed Bo to be rude. It wasn't in her DNA to turn a cold shoulder to anyone, but this situation was *way* outside of normal. How could she possibly fall for someone that was using her and her father for his own benefit? She had no idea what he needed her father for, but she assumed it was for no good.

Though, even given the circumstances, Bo's animosity was grudgingly fading every day. It also didn't help that with every meal, he'd bring her a new pile of books to read. As well as the fact that at least once a day he'd enter her room in different states of undress. Showing off his incredible physique. Bo was quickly losing her resolve and needed to get the hell out of there quickly.

Finally, after a week, a miracle presented itself in the form of Roc's sweet old maid. The knock at the door at an odd time of day startled Bo as she read one of the books Roc had loaned her. Expecting Roc to walk in, Bo was surprised to see the tiny older woman come through the door.

"Hello, Miss Cabrera." The maid greeted her. "Mr. Bennett told me to come gather your sheets and whatever items you need washed," she informed her.

"Uh, sure." Bo hesitated, not believing her luck.

"I'm Betty. I help Mr. Bennett clean up around here." Betty introduced herself as she walked over to where Bo was sitting.

"Well thanks, Betty. And just call me Bo." The pretty Latina offered as she gently shook the woman's work-roughened hands.

Bo quickly rose from the chaise lounge in front of the huge barred picture window. She grabbed her dirty clothes out of the bedroom hamper and handed them to the woman. Her eyes continually going to the unlocked door as Betty removed the sheets from the king size bed.

As was her habit, Bo overthought her plan of action and missed her window of opportunity as Betty put on a new set of sheets. The older woman grabbed her now full laundry basket and headed for the bedroom door. Bo mentally bashed her head against the wall for taking too long to make a move. Though, just when she thought all was lost, Betty stopped short.

"Darn it! I almost forgot to grab your dirty bath towels. I tell you, I'm getting forgetful in my old age." Betty berated herself as she made her way into the en-suite.

The moment Betty disappeared into the bathroom, Bo took off. She leapt over the laundry basket in front of the door and ran out into the hallway. She had no idea where she was going, considering Roc had carried her into her temporary prison cell, when she was passed out.

Bo's heart pounded as she ran down the long hallway. She eventually found the large staircase that lead to the foyer and front door. She didn't give herself time to think or talk herself out of escaping. Bo just barreled down the stairs and burst out the front door.

She heard the faint shout of Betty's voice calling her name from where she had come. In a panic Bo ran cross the driveway and through the yard. Luck was in her favor when she spotted a ladder lying down in the grass, near the high walls that surrounded the perimeter of the house. Bo realized that the gardener or someone must have left it. She thanked Roc's house staff for being so helpful in her escape.

Bo grasped the ladder, lifted it up, and placed it against the wall. She quickly clambered up the ladder to the top of the wall. Once she was on top and looked down on the other side a wave of vertigo hit her. She knew that there was no way that she was going to jump from that high up. So with all of the strength she could muster, Bo pulled the ladder up from one side and lowered it on the other. To the side of her eminent freedom.

She quickly made her way down and took off into the woods. She realized too late that she had brought nothing with her. She had no food or water, no extra clothes and no coat. The evening air up in the mountains was cool and she knew would soon turn cold. But she also knew that the only alternative was to go back. Bo hoped that she could find another house along the way.

Her lungs burned from running and her stomach and legs were cramping from the effort. *I sure did chose a fine time to become active.* She slowed down to a brisk walk and she tried to ignore the sounds and shadows the forest emitted along the way. Fear was the last thing she needed. Though, the emotion crept up on her anyway. The woods quickly became alarmingly dark and with no light to guide her way, Bo started to trip over downed tree limbs and tangled underbrush.

"Dammit! I would've been better off waiting till I could get his car keys. Don't freak out, Bo. Don't freak out." She started chanting to herself.

Just then, Bo's foot caught on something and she stumbled forward. The momentum sent her tumbling head over feet down a small hill. Luckily she didn't hurt anything vital. When she finally came to a stop, she shook her head, more disoriented than anything.

When her jumbled vision cleared, the light of the half-moon shown down faintly through the break in the trees. Only a few feet away from her, Bo could see the shadow and reflective eyes of a large animal. Her heartbeat broke out into a sprint and she could barely hear anything above the sound of blood roaring in her ears.

The glowing eyes moved as if the creature was stalking her, waiting for the perfect opening. Its body coiled tight and then sprang forward towards the cowering woman. A roar that was not the blood rushing in her ears, came from the right of Bo. She saw an equally, if not bigger shadow, leap onto the other. She could only really hear the fight taking place a few feet from her. The sound of a large cat cried out and then there was silence.

A moment later, a huge hulking shadow stood over her. Bo instinctively knew in her heart that it was Roc, though she couldn't see him. She didn't know whether to be relieved or terrified.

"Come." Roc said quietly. The one word saying volumes. Bo could hear the restrained anger behind it.

He reached for her hand and pulled her up. Though, Bo had no idea how he could even see her in the darkness. He flung her onto his back and she held on like a Spider monkey. He grunted slightly as if in pain and then started jogging easily back to his home with her on his back. Bo was stunned by his strength, agility, and ability to see in the pitch black forest. Though, she held back her commentary and just tried to hold on for dear life.

~~~

Roc was furious, but he refused to say anything. He was afraid that he might lash out at Bo harshly. When he had heard Betty calling out his name, he'd run from his study to see what was wrong. The minute Betty explained the situation, Roc barely let her finish before he was out the door and running full speed towards the scent Bo left behind.

He had been scared out of his mind that she would hurt herself in the dark woods. If she wasn't attacked by any number of predators, he had been worried that she would break her fool neck, tripping in the dark. He growled deeply thinking about how she had nearly accomplished both at the same time.

Roc had just caught up with her when she'd tumbled down the hill and had almost gotten eaten alive by a mountain lion. The last thing he had really wanted to do was kill the big cat, but he didn't have much choice in the matter. And now, it took all of his restraint not to shake some sense into her.

He jogged up to the opened gate to his property and he realized that Betty must have opened it for him. Roc continued on with Bo on his back, until he finally walked through the front door where Betty awaited them. He let Bo slide down from his back. The second her feet touched the ground, he grabbed her wrist in a tight restraining hold, keeping her next to him.

"Everything is fine, Betty. You can go home now. Just finish the rest tomorrow." Roc instructed.

"No problem, Mr. Bennett. I'm glad you found her. Though you look like you been attacked by a she-cat." Betty frowned in concern.

"You have no idea. But I'm fine Betty," he said sweetly to the older woman. "Bo, please apologize to Betty for scaring her senseless." Roc ground out, his tone changed to barely concealed anger when he addressed her.

"Sorry, Betty." Bo said in a small voice.

"Oh, don't worry about it. I'm just happy you're safe." Betty patted Bo's arm and headed out the door. Bo doubted the woman's words. *Safe wouldn't be the word I'd go with.*

The moment the door closed, Roc started towards the stairs. He pulled Bo along behind him and she struggled to keep up with his long strides. She wished that the older woman would have stayed to protect her from Roc's wrath.

Roc lead her down the hall, back to her bedroom. He pulled her roughly into the room and flung her away from him as if in disgust. Bo stumbled towards the bed and then turned to look at him clearly for the first time after he'd saved her.

Roc's shirt was torn to shreds and blood stained the fabric. Fresh scratches marred his beautiful dark skin. Bo immediately felt contrite over what she had done.

"You're bleeding." Bo said softly as she reached out hesitantly.

Roc flinched away from her and her two words set off his hair trigger. "What the fuck were you thinking?!" Roc bellowed.

"I don't know." Bo whispered as she cringed away from his fury.

"What?!" Roc shouted when he couldn't hear her softly spoken words.

"I don't know!" Bo screamed back.

"Well that's a piss poor excuse. You were nearly killed for God's sake!" Roc growled as he stalked towards her and invaded her space.

Bo's butt hit the mattress and she leaned back over it, trying to keep her distance from the gorgeous, angry man.

"I'm gonna ask you again. What were you thinking?" Roc asked, his warm breath fanned her already flushed skin.

"I-I wanted to es-escape. I didn't think about anything else." Bo admitted as she turned her face away from his. Afraid that in his close proximity she'd be tempted to finally see what his lips felt like.

"Why?" Roc asked and Bo knew what the one word question was in reference to.

"B-Because I d-didn't want you t-to wear me d-down." Bo confessed haltingly.

"Wear you down?" Roc asked in confusion.

"T-Tempt me." Bo added.

Realization hit Roc then. Bo finally looked up at him, her eyes asking what her lips refused to speak. Neither one of them could say who reached for who first. Just one minute they were staring at each other and the next, Bo's lips were crushed against Roc's.

Roc held her face tightly between his large hands as he devoured her plump lips. His tongue stroked aggressively into her warm, wet mouth. She shuddered every time his tongue flicked against hers.

Bo had been right, his lips were like soft, plush pillows. She had never been kissed the way Roc was kissing her now. His passion felt overwhelming. Yet at the same time it matched the need that he brought out of her. Bo had never considered herself a passionate person, until this very moment.

Her trembling, urgent hands went to Roc's shredded t-shirt. Bo had been desperate to touch his rich, dark skin for days and she didn't hesitate to touch him now. She pulled up the shirt and her fingers stroked his smooth skin. It almost felt like his heat singed her fingertips.

Roc released her lips long enough to let her pull the shirt up over his head. The moment his head was clear of the torn fabric, he was back again at her small, plump lips. His massive hands roamed the soft contours of her body. In his need to feel her creamy tan skin, Roc accidentally ripped Bo's clothing in half, trying to hastily remove them. He hadn't had sex in five years and his overly anxious and trembling fingers gave him away.

Bo reached back and unclasped her bra, helping his clumsy fingers. When her breast were free from their bindings, Roc bent down to taste and kiss their dark tips. His tongue swirled around each peak, turning them into stiff little nubs. Bo's hips reflexively pumped towards the empty space between them, seeking out the most intimate part of Roc's body. Begging to be filled.

Roc answered the call of her body, his equally straining to get to her wet warmth. He became delirious in his need. Roc ripped her panties away and quickly lifted her butt to the edge of the bed. He unzipped his jeans and pushed them and his briefs down far enough to release his pulsating steel. Roc captured Bo's lips in a searing kiss. At the same time that his tongue stroked into her mouth, his aching cock that was poised at her entrance, plunged into her awaiting heat.

Unprepared for the sheer size of his hard, wide length, Bo cried out in shock. She wasn't a virgin, but she had been with only one other lover and it had been two years ago. Her ex didn't compare to this beast of a man and her body responded instantly.

Roc held still long enough for her body to relax around him. Once she was ready, Roc pulled back out to the rim of his mushroom cap and stroked back in deeply. Bo's back arched off the bed and she choked on a cry caught in her throat. Roc wrapped one arm around her lower back and his other hand wrapped around the back of her neck. He pulled her towards him till they were forehead to forehead. And with the leverage of his arm around her waist, he pumped into her slick folds over and over again.

Bo reached for the hard flexing roundness of Roc's ass, in her need to hold onto something as he thrust powerfully into her. The built up tension in her tummy felt like it would drive her mad. Just then, Roc rolled his hips on an inward stroke and Bo's body tightened like a coil. And with one more rolling pump, the coil released. Roc covered her mouth with a deep kiss as she screamed.

Roc stopped his movements as Bo came apart in his arms. Her body convulsed with spasms and her legs trembled uncontrollably. Roc had every intention of continuing when her climax subsided, but the powerful contractions of her pussy around his throbbing manhood milked an unexpected orgasm out of him. His cum spilled into her awaiting womb. Roc instantly knew his mistake after the delirium passed.

"I'm so sorry." Roc groaned against Bo's belly after he collapsed on top of her.

"What's wrong? That was wonderful." Bo said looking down as she stroked his smooth bald head.

All Roc could think of, was Bo getting pregnant with a child infected with his curse. It wouldn't be fair to her or the child. He felt sick to his stomach because of his carelessness.

"I didn't wear any protection and I didn't pull out." Roc said disgusted with himself.

"It's okay." Bo soothed.

"You don't know what you're saying. You don't want my offspring." Roc said sadly.

"No, I mean that I got the birth control shot with my last boyfriend and have been on it ever since. I'm surprised you didn't know that, considering your stalker tendencies. So you're telling me that you didn't get my medical records too?" Bo teased him, showing her playful side for the first time.

"No, I didn't take it that far, but thank God. That could've been a disaster." Roc blew out a relieved breath.

"Not that I'm ready for motherhood, but what would be so terrible about having your babies?" Bo asked perplexed.

Roc raised up on his forearms and peppered soft kisses on her breasts as he tried to stall for time. He didn't know if he was ready to tell her about his curse. He didn't want to see the disgust or fear on her face. Or the look in her eyes, if she didn't believe him and thought he was crazy. His love for her had only grown once he got a chance to witness her passion and fire, firsthand. It would kill him if she turned her back on him.

"You can tell me. I promise I won't judge." Bo encouraged as she crawled backwards to the middle of the bed and patted the space next to her. Roc followed her and laid his head on her chest, so he wouldn't have to look at the reactions that would cross her face.

"I doubt you'll feel that way after you hear what I have to say." Roc said as he took a deep breath before plowing ahead. "I'm cursed…"

Bo stroked her hand down his head, neck and shoulders while she listened to his story. At the more shocking parts of his story, her hand would stop or hesitate and her heart rate would pick up. But other than that, she didn't pull away from him or stop affectionately caressing him.

She thought that his story seemed impossible. *There's no such thing as werewolves.* But the scars on his face and the desperation in his crazy scheme involving Bo and her father made his story seem plausible. Not to mention the fact that his cuts and scratches from the mountain lion had completely healed within the timeframe it took for him to make love to her.

"My dad will help you. I'm sure of it." Bo said confidently.

Roc's head popped up from her chest in surprise. His beautiful dark eyes were wide with disbelief.

"You believe me?" He asked.

"Yes. I mean, I don't see why else you'd go to such drastic measures." Bo reasoned.

"And you're not scared of me?" He continued on.

"No." Bo answered without hesitation.

"How is that possible?"

"Well I mean, right now you look like a beautiful man to me. Maybe I'd feel differently if I saw you change, but in this moment you're perfect." Bo ended bashfully.

"I don't deserve that type of praise." Roc shook his head. "I haven't been the greatest person and I'm not worthy of your level of perfection. But I would do anything to be the man you deserve." He finished earnestly.

Bo's eyes immediately filled with tears. No man had ever spoken to her so passionately before. She was overwhelmed by the deep connection she felt between them. She reached for Roc's face and pulled him down to her. His soft lips felt heavenly against hers. Instantly she felt the heat resurge through her body. Bo surprised herself and Roc when she quickly whipped around, pushed Roc's back down onto the mattress and straddled his hips.

She slid her wet labia up and down his quickly hardening shaft. Bo looked down at his massive, dark chocolate appendage, slick with her arousal, and swallowed hard. *Holy shit!!! How did I fit him inside of me the first time?!*

Bo leaned forward and flicked her tongue against his nipple and watched as the dark flat disk puckered under her attentions. Roc pulled her towards his face and raised his head to taste her sweet mouth. Bo's hair fell like a dark curtain around them. She broke the kiss on a gasp and sat up, placing her hands on his sculpted chest.

Bo raised her hips and clasped Roc's thick cock, positioning him at her entrance. Slowly she slid down his length, letting him stretch her beyond capacity. The new angle on top, brought him deeper than before and she whimpered as her body tried to accommodate him. All the while, they held eye contact. She bit down on her lip and released it on a cry, her mouth parted and wet.

Roc gazed up at her in awe. She was literally the most beautiful thing he had ever seen. And he couldn't find a single solitary reason why she wouldn't have appealed to him in the past. She was magnificent.

"My Bonita." Roc breathed. "So beautiful. You fit your name perfectly."

He reached up to cup the side of her face gently. Bo clutched his hand tightly as she continued to slide up and down his erection. Her long, ebony locks spilled over onto one breast and her eyes were heavy-lidded and sultry. Roc thought she looked made for this, made for passion. Mild-mannered bookworm, she was not.

Adding to her overall seduction, Bo clasped his large hand and pulled it towards her mouth. She slowly opened her mouth and flicked her tongue against the pad of his thumb. She then drew Roc's thumb into her mouth, sucking him. And finally, she bit down on it, baring her teeth.

Roc lost it in that moment. He pulled his hand away from her delectable mouth, he gripped her wide hips to hold her still, and then he pounded upward with punishing strokes. Bo's head fell back and he could feel her hair brushing his thighs as he fucked her hard.

Her full, little breasts bounced with every thrust and her thick thighs rippled. The vision of her alone tightened his scrotum, ready to explode inside of her. Roc doubled his efforts, wanting her to come with him. Bo reached back to grip his thighs and dug her nails in as her climax washed over her.

"Roc!" She screamed as her walls milked him.

"Fuck! Bo!" He shouted out as he quickly followed her to euphoria.

Bo collapsed onto Roc's chest. He stroked his fingertips delicately over her soft back and they both drifted off into a blissful sleep.

~~~

The next three weeks were enchanting for Bo and Roc. Bo contacted her father and let him know that she was staying of her own freewill. Miguel wasn't ecstatic over the turn of events, but he was happy that Roc seemed to be treating her well.

They spent days in bed. They explored each other physically and mentally. Tasting, touching, and talking for hours. Though, as each day drew nearer to the approaching full moon, they became more and more anxious.

Miguel still hadn't found the cure to Roc's curse. Roc was trying to decide what he was going to do with Bo. He didn't want her anywhere near him when he changed. He knew he'd never forgive himself if he hurt her.

"I need you to go stay with your father for a day or two." Roc said the night before the full moon.

"I won't leave you." Bo said defiantly.

"You have to. I couldn't live with myself if something happened to you." Roc reasoned.

"It might not even be what you think it is. You don't even know what happens to you and no one has ever seen it." Bo said.

"Exactly the point! If anyone saw it, they didn't live to tell about it!" Roc rubbed his smooth head in frustration.

"Maybe I could stop you. What if I chain you to the bed and then we could wait it out till morning?" Bo suggested.

"I don't know, Bo. It's too risky." Roc grimaced with indecision.

"Please, Roc. Let me stay." Bo pleaded with him.

Roc thought hard for several minutes, before finally answering. "Alright. But I'm going to give you a gun and if I escape from the chains, you have to use it." Roc compromised.

"Okay. I will."

~~~

The next evening, Roc laid in the middle of the bed and watched as Bo secured his ankles with a heavy shackle. There were two chains that had a shackle on each end. Before laying in the bed, Roc placed the heavy chains under the foot and head of the bed.

Roc's eyes filled with worry as they followed Bo to the side of the bed. She locked his right wrist in the heavy metal restraint. Bo crawled onto the bed, intending to crawl over him to the other side to lock his left wrist. Though, before she could get there, Roc's left hand shot out to grasp her forearm. His eyes searched hers for a moment, as if he was memorizing her face for the last time.

"Don't forget. If I break free you have to kill me." Roc said, his voice filled with desperation.

"Alright. I won't forget." Bo said sadly.

With his one free arm, Roc pulled her closer to him and kissed her hard and quick. "Okay, hurry before the sun goes down."

Bo quickly scrambled to the other side of the bed and placed the last restraint around his wrist. Once she was done, Bo walked over to the chaise lounge and the gun loaded with silver bullets that sat on the coffee table. She sat down facing the bed, the last vestiges of the sun's rays shining through the window. The light behind her cast her in silhouette and to Roc she looked like an angel waiting to take him to heaven. He prayed that that wouldn't be the case.

The sun finally reached its descent as the white round glow of her sister rose high in the sky. Bo turned on the table lamp and Roc brought his head up one more time to look at her.

"I love you." Roc said for the first time to anyone.

A sharp pain ripped through his body and he shouted and strained against his bonds. Bo watched in fear and fascination as his body bucked and convulsed against the bed. She quickly reached for the gun and clutched it tightly in her trembling hands.

An inhuman growl tore from his throat and Bo slowly stood up, hypnotized by the change happening before her eyes. Roc's eyes were clenched shut and then they flew open. No longer were they the warm dark brown she was used to, now they were a glowing gold. His already large muscles grew before her eyes, ripping through his clothes. Fur sprouted from invisible follicles on his mahogany skin.

This sight rose goosebumps across her skin and made her skin itch. Last, she heard what sounded like bones breaking and watched as a wolf's snout formed from Roc's once beautiful full lips.

The gun shook uncontrollably in her hand and her heart raced harder than she'd ever felt before. She could barely breathe from the fear that was choking her. The straining muscles in his now even more powerful arm and legs, snapped the shackles like toothpicks.

The beast that had taken over Roc's body, lithely jumped up and crouched in the middle of the mattress and stared at her. Bo raised her shaking hands and attempted to point the gun at him. Her aim was so erratic that she was sure that she would miss if she did pull the trigger. *Dear God, I can't do it! I can't do it.*

Tears streamed down Bo's face. She knew that her life was about to end, but she couldn't shoot him. No matter how hard she tried. His muscles bunched and coiled ready to spring into action. A low growl rumbled in his chest and he snarled, showing off gleaming white fangs. There was no man left in the creature before her.

Bo lowered the gun and it fell to the floor at her feet. As he sprang forward, she closed her eyes. Ready. And she spoke three words.

"I love you."

She squeezed her eyes tight as she waited for the attack. But all she heard was a heavy thump. A bright light pierced through the thin skin of her eyelids. Bo's eyes flew open and the beast was surrounded by a blinding light as he lie on the floor. And she watched as he slowly changed back to his human form.

Once more, Bo could see his beautiful, smooth ebony skin. His muscles had receded back to their regular size. And his eyes opened to their natural warm brown as the light around him ebbed.

Roc shook his head and slowly looked up at Bo. His face changed from confusion to joyful wonder, as he stared at her. "You're still alive! Wait…and so am I. What day is it?" Roc asked perplexed.

"It's only been a few minutes." Bo said with tears running down her face.

"What?! What happened?" Roc asked in shock.

"I-I think the curse is broken." Bo said with a shaky voice as she stepped closer to him, afraid to believe it was true.

"How?" Roc asked in awe as he slowly stood up, not caring that he was as naked as the day he was born.

"You broke through your chains like they were twigs. And you were about to attack me when I said, 'I love you'. Then you fell to the floor and a bright light surrounded you as you changed back to your human form." Bo explained.

"You love me?" Roc asked shyly. He realized the key all along to breaking his curse was not her father and science, but the quiet yet passionate librarian and her love.

"Y-Yes," Bo said still trembling with roiling emotions.

"I'm so sorry I put you through that." Roc said reaching out for her once he saw the tremors running through her.

Bo let him pull her into the strong circle of his arms. She looked up at him with watery eyes and Roc gently wiped away the tears from her cheeks with his thumbs. He then started to plant happy kisses all over Bo's face until her nerves subsided and she started to giggle.

"You saved my life." Roc said seriously, once he stopped kissing her. "How will I ever repay you?"

Bo lifted her arms in front of her, palms up, with her wrists together. "Keep me captive…forever."

Roc pulled the sheet off of the bed, twisted it till it became a makeshift rope, and then tied one end around her wrists. He guided her to the bed, laid her down in the middle, and tied the other end to the bedframe. Crawling onto the bed with her, Roc ripped her shirt apart with his bare hands and pulled her jeans and panties down and off her plump, shapely legs. Then he leaned down to flick her lips with his wet tongue. Bo gasped and her hips pumped up reflexively.

 Roc crawled down her body and placed her legs over his shoulders. He looked up at her and grinned rakishly. "Gladly." He said softly before lowering his head.

••••

Slumber

Ro Montgomery was headed back from her Dirty Thirty birthday celebration. She and her best friend, Mary had hailed a cab outside of a bar on Rush St. in downtown Chicago. They were now singing along to *You Oughta Know* at the top of their lungs, in the backseat. It had been more than just a birthday party but also a 'Fuck Mark' party too. Mary had been heartbroken when her boyfriend of seven years had broken up with her the week before. He had told her that he'd missed most of his twenties while dating her and wanted to see other women before he had to settle down.

So to end the night, Ro had pulled up the ultimate 'fuck you' song and they laughingly slurred the iconic lyrics. A nice haze of alcohol surrounded them and made their heads fuzzy. They didn't see the drunk driver that blew through the red light and T-boned their taxi.

~~~

Dr. Flip Harris made his final rounds of the Neuro-ICU unit at Chicago Medical Center. He checked his patient's charts and chatted with those who were awake. He saved *her* room for last.

Flip walked into the room and as always his heart thudded thickly in his chest. Ro Montgomery was the most beautiful woman he had ever seen. She had gorgeous, golden wavy locks that stopped at the middle of her back. Her little nose was pert and slightly upturned, above small full lips. She had beautiful, almond-shaped hazel eyes. Though he had only seen them when he lifted her eyelid to check her pupils, after she'd first arrived at the ER in an ambulance.

Ro's body was soft and full. Her skin was slightly kissed by the summer sun. Flip had seen beautiful women his whole life and were chased by quite a few. Though something about this girl touched him the moment her gurney had burst through the ER doors.

Her, her friend and their taxi driver had been hit by a drunk driver. Miraculously they had all survived. Mary had a broken leg and arm, and the taxi driver had had internal bleeding that they'd sewn up. The drunk driver, as always, came away with only minor cuts and bruises.

Mary was released the next day when all her tests had come back clear. The cab driver was released about a week ago. And the drunk driver was also released the day after the accident and sent straight to jail.

Ro, unfortunately, had not been so lucky. When she'd come in, beyond the cuts and bruises, it didn't look like there was anything wrong with her. Aside from the fact that she was unresponsive. Which was why they paged Flip, knowing they were going to need a neurosurgeon after her eye exam looked troubling.

Flip had lifted each eyelid and flashed his otoscope in each of her pupils and he saw that she'd had swelling of the optic nerve. They quickly rushed her to get a CT scan. The results had shown that she'd had a brain bleed. They had immediately wheeled her into an available OR.

He knew that the surgery had went well. Flawless, in fact. She'd had swelling and they put her in a medically induced coma to stop the edema, before it did major damage. After her surgery, the swelling had gone down and her vitals were stable. Everything was textbook perfect but after two weeks, Ro still wasn't coming out of her coma.

Flip looked down at her, his frustrations mounting with each passing day. "Dammit! Why won't you wake up? Where did I go wrong?" Flip growled, angry at himself.

"Doctor?" A voice came from the doorway.

Flip turned to see Ro's best friend, Mary. He cringed knowing that she more than likely had heard his rant.

"Sorry, Ms. Ferris." Flip apologized.

"No changes, huh?" Mary asked solemnly, hobbling in awkwardly. Both her left leg and arm were set in hot pink casts.

"No, unfortunately not." Flip sighed as he sat on the edge of the bed. "The surgery went well. *Very* well. Her vitals are perfect but she's just not waking up." He explained.

He wrapped his long graceful fingers, surgeon's fingers, around Ro's wrist and checked her pulse. It, of course, was strong and sure. *I just don't get it.* He thought to himself.

"It'll work itself out, I'm sure." Mary comforted him, in a strange role reversal. "She'll come around. Maybe she's just milking it." She grinned and then leaned over the bed to talk to Ro. "I know you needed a vacation, but jeez!" Mary joked and then swallowed thickly, obviously more worried than she was let on.

Flip chuckled reluctantly at the joke. "I'll give you some privacy."

"Thanks." Mary said sadly before he left the room.

~~~

"Haha! Very funny, Mary. I'm here, I swear! I can hear you! Don't let the doctor leave!" Ro screamed uselessly.

She had been trapped in a room with no doors. Only a vintage chaise lounge and an elaborate chandelier hanging from above. She'd been there for the last two weeks, since the accident. At least she thought it was that long. The sparkling chandelier was her only source of light, since the room didn't have any windows either. So she had no concept of time. Though she could hear anyone that came to speak to her. Almost like a cruel joke.

She was terrified that she'd go mad if they didn't help her soon.

"We'll find a way to get you out of this coma, Ro. I promise." She heard Mary say as if from a tunnel.

"Please hurry, Mary! Please, hurry." Ro collapsed on the lounge and started to sob.

~~~

Flip desolately made is way from the hospital to the Children's hospital's annual carnival fundraiser being held at Navy Pier. Many of the sick or recovering children, their families, and the general public were enjoying the festivities.

There were rides, booths with games to win stuffed animals, and vendors' booths that sold their wares. There was even a dunk tank, where the kids could dunk their doctors and nurses, when they arrived before or after their shifts for the day. Everyone was in high spirits, except for Flip.

He made his way around, stopping to talk with everyone. He smiled when it was polite, but his mind was never far from the quiet hospital room. Where a beauty slept and wouldn't wake up.

As usual the women who were in attendance, stared at him longingly. Almost sighing as he passed by. Flip was beyond gorgeous to the majority of women he came across. His mother being Chinese and his father black, his skin was a caramely brown. His dark hair was cut low but long enough on top to showcase adorable tight curls. His brown eyes, he got from his mother, were warm yet seductive and his full lips begged to be kissed. Flip's body, like his father; was tall, broad, and muscular. He'd played college football and was good enough to go pro, but chose the academic route instead. And he'd become a brilliant neurosurgeon, though he still kept his body in near perfect, football condition.

His physical appearance, his sharp mind, -and let's face it- his bank account; all combined to make him one of the greatest catches in all of Chicago. Though he hadn't been looking to get caught lately.

Flip had dated several women over the years. Too many to count, in fact. Most of them had been socialites or wannabes that unfortunately circulated around his world. Flip had become tired, fairly quickly, of the grasping materialistic, often empty-headed, gold-diggers that came into his life. So he'd taken a much needed vacation from dating nearly a year ago. Which was why he didn't see the looks of attraction, lust, and adoration as he passed by the women at the carnival.

"It's not a coma. It's an ill wish." A gravely voice reached his ears.

Flip stopped and looked around, but he only saw a little old woman with a gypsy-like turban on her head. She wore a voluminous and shapeless dress, along with several rings on each finger. Her booth was draped in bright silky scarves and cloth. One in deep purple hung over a round table with the cliché crystal ball on top.

The supposed fortune teller looked directly at him, so Flip assumed she had been addressing him as he passed.

"Excuse me?" He asked hesitantly.

"It's not a coma. It's an ill wish." The woman repeated.

Flip stepped closer to the woman, curious. "What do you mean?"

"The beauty you're fretting over. She is not in a coma. She's under a…let's say, a spell." The old woman informed him.

"A spell? Like a fairy tale?" Flip said skeptically.

"I guess you could say that." The woman nodded and shrugged her shoulders.

"Yeah. O….kay." Flip said, his voice filled with sarcasm as he started to turn and walk away.

"I know you don't believe me." The woman blurted out and clasped his arm tightly. Stronger than he would've imagined for such a little woman. "But you should. Modern medicine can't save her. Though you can if you take a chance."

"I'm listening." Flip said with a doubtful scowl.

"Her grandfather broke the heart of a dangerous woman, years ago. So she put a curse on him and his entire bloodline." The fortune teller explained with a faraway look in her eyes. "Great tragedy will befall every member of his family by their thirtieth birthday. If you don't believe me, check her family history and you'll see." The gypsy finished.

"Well, even if I were to believe you. What can I do about it, if medicine won't cure her?" Flip asked in frustration.

"In order to save her, you must go in and bring her back." The old woman informed him.

"Go in where? I already went into her brain to fix it. Where else can I go?" Flip asked in confusion.

"I'm not talking about the physical world. There are other dimensions that you don't even know about. She is currently trapped in one of them. So you need to go in and find her." She said firmly.

"How in the hell am I supposed to go to another dimension to find her?" Flip was starting to lose his patience with the silly discussion.

The old woman dug around in a bag she had next to her. She pulled something out that was clutched in her hand and she said a few words in another language that Flip didn't understand. She then held her hand out facing down, waiting for him to hold out his.

Flip slid his hand across the table, palm up. She opened her fingers and a blue crystal with a leather cord tied around it, dropped into his hand.

"Put this around your neck. Go to her room, take her hand and say, 'I am of this world. World fall away and take me to her.' Repeat this as you fall asleep and you'll reach her dimension. Though, I must warn you." The old woman paused for effect and Flip leaned in curiously. "It won't be easy. You'll have to fight off your worst fears to get to her. But if you do, you'll be worthy of her. Of her love. And if you bring her back, you'll also break the curse. The decision is yours." The gypsy finished.

"Uh…thanks. I think." Flip said as he rose up from the table still clutching the crystal pendant.

"Still don't believe me, ask her friend Mary about her family." The old woman called out as he strode away.

Flip had been ready to discount everything the fortune teller had said. As soon as he was out of her line of sight, he was going to pitch the necklace in the trash. Though, her parting words stopped him. It was impossible for her to know that Ro had a friend named Mary. It was impossible for her to know a lot of what she'd said.

He rushed back to the hospital in the hopes that Mary would still be there visiting Ro. He strode swiftly into the building, greeting colleagues quickly as he passed by. He practically ran to Ro's room and skidded to a halt at the door. He was in luck, Mary was still there.

"Mary!" Flip said breathless. "I have to ask you something."

"Uh, sure Doc. What's up?" The slender brunette asked.

"Ro is thirty, right?"

"Yes."

"When did she turn thirty?"

"The night of the accident."

Flip swallowed hard.

"Where are her parents? Why haven't they come to visit her?" He asked warily.

"Oh, they both passed away years ago. Her dad was in some sort of boating accident and died. They think her mother died of a broken heart after that. My family lived next door to them, so my parents decided to take Ro in and raise her." Mary told him sadly.

"Do you know how old her father was when he died?" Flip asked hesitantly.

"I'm pretty sure he was twenty-nine." Mary nodded.

"She has no aunts or uncles or grandparents?"

"No, they all died in terrible accidents. Ro has never really said it out loud, but I think she thinks her family is cursed." Mary said as she squeezed Ro's limp hand.

"Did they all die by the age of thirty?" Flip asked nervously.

"Um… Oh God! I think they did. You don't think…" Mary left the question in the air, not willing to say it out loud.

"I don't know. But it's not looking good." Flip said rubbing his hand across his forehead roughly.

"I-If it is a curse, does that mean she won't ever wake up?" Mary said fearfully.

"I don't know. But I intend to do everything in my power not to let that happen." Flip said with determination.

Ro could hear the entire conversation between the doctor and her best friend. She sat cross-legged on the lounge with her face in her hands as she rocked back and forth. She had no idea how the doctor was going to try to pull her out of whatever state she was in.

She had known or at least had a feeling that her family was cursed. But she had no idea why. She wondered how the doctor knew enough about her supposed curse, to ask Mary questions about it. He apparently knew more than she did.

"God, help me." Ro said desperately.

She had no idea how much longer she could take being trapped in her current state of mental solitary confinement.

~~~

Flip ran home to his high rise condo to plan and prepare for that evening. He knew that he couldn't do what the fortune teller had told him to do, in the hospital. With the nurses doing their rounds, they would definitely notice him sleeping next to the comatose woman. Which wasn't normal behavior for a doctor.

On his way home from the hospital, he'd snatched a release form. He filled out the form, intending to leave it at the nurses' desk when he went back to the hospital. So that after he took Ro, and the nurse on the nightshift did her rounds and saw the empty room, she'd go and find the release form signed by him. No one would be the wiser.

Flip quickly ate, showered, and then got dressed. He threw on a pair of relaxed fit jeans, a gray hooded sweatshirt for the cool summer night, and a pair of white gym shoes. He left his building and drove the few blocks to the hospital in his black jeep. Once he arrived at the hospital, he was able to get by the main front desk on the first floor with just a nod. Though his floor wasn't going to be so easy.

"Hey, Dr. Harris! What are you doing here this evening? I didn't think you'd be back till morning." One of the nurses said as he tried to pass by.

"Hi, Claudia." Flip greeted, letting a brilliant smile spread across his face. The nurse instantly melted like butter under the force of his sunny smile. *Checkmate.* "I'm a little bothered about this patient that won't wake up. So I just thought I'd come check on her one more time before I go home for the night." He explained.

"Oh, yes. I'm so sorry to hear about your patient. I'm sure she'll come around though. You're a phenomenal surgeon, after all," she said as she batted her eyelashes at him.

"Thanks, Claudia. Well, I'll talk to ya later." Flip said as he made his way to Ro's hospital room.

He walked into the room and she looked the same as every time he'd come in to check on her. She hadn't moved an inch and her eyes were still firmly closed. Flip walked to her bed and reached for her soft hand.

"I will bring you out of this, I promise." Flip whispered.

Flip walked back to the door and snuck a peek out, looking in either direction. No nurses were lurking about, so he quickly strode to the end of the hall where a wheelchair was parked. He took the breaks off of the wheels and rolled it down the hall.

Once he was back in the hospital room, Flip slid his hands under Ro's back and knees and lifted her out of the bed. He gently placed her in the wheelchair. He unhooked the bag of intravenous food that hung on the metal stand and placed it in her lap, along with her personal items collected from the accident. He grabbed the white hospital blanket and threw it over her lap and up around her shoulders. Flip wheeled her to the doorway and peeked out again. There wasn't a nurse in sight, so Flip took off. As he passed the nurses desk, he slipped the release form in the bin designated for the forms. He then rolled her to the elevators and brought her down to the lower level without a hitch.

Flip wheeled her outside and quickly got her in the passenger seat of his jeep. He strapped her in and her head lolled limply on her chest. Flip walked to the other side of the car and hopped into the driver's seat. He looked over at Ro's unconscious body as he started the car.

"I don't know if this'll work, but I have to try." Flip said and took off down the street.

~~~

"Thank you." Ro said to the doctor, though she knew he couldn't hear her.

She paced the near empty room, from one side to the other. She was anxious to see if whatever plan he had cooked up would work. She prayed that it did because she was going stir crazy and she knew it hadn't even been that long since she'd been under the spell. Or whatever it was that was wrong with her.

Ro's life had been textbook. At a young age she knew that something wasn't right. She'd realized that all of her family didn't make it past thirty. So in her mind she thought that being perfect; getting good grades, dating the nice boy that she never got too close to, and having a respectable teaching career would change her stars.

Each year that brought her closer to thirty, scared her half to death. Most women were freaking out about turning thirty because they all of a sudden felt old. Like their life was over. She *knew* that there was a very good chance that her life *would* be over at thirty.

When she woke up on her birthday still alive, she thought that maybe she had beat the odds. Maybe the curse had dwindled over the years, lost its steam. Maybe she was different. She was not.

~~~

Flip laid her gently in his king size bed. He looked down at Ro and took a deep breath. He was a man of science. He didn't believe in this hokey, mumbo jumbo. Though every time he tried to explain how the fortune teller knew what she did, he couldn't. He was desperate to help Ro. He even felt a strange obsession coming over him. Like he knew her, or at least wanted to.

He whipped off his sweatshirt and kicked off his shoes. Leaving on his white tank and jeans, Flip crawled into bed with her. He clasped Ro's cool, dry hand with his warm and sweaty one. The crystal pendant was already around his neck and he adjusted it to lie in the middle of his solid chest.

Flip took another deep breath and then closed his eyes. He easily pulled up the phrase the gypsy had given him and started to repeat if over and over again.

"I am of this world. World fall away and take me to her. I am of this…"

As Flip drifted off to sleep the blue crystal changed to pink and began to glow brightly on his chest.

~~~

Flip opened his eyes and saw the night sky above him. The stars that twinkled in the inky blackness seemed brighter than normal. He looked to either side of him and Ro was no longer there and he wasn't in his bed either. He was lying on the grass someplace unknown. He quickly sat up and before him was a giant wall of green shrubs with only one opening. He assessed the situation and realized immediately that it was the opening to a maze. How big the maze was, he couldn't tell. Not with the wall of greenery being at least ten feet tall.

He looked all around him to see if there was any other way, besides forward. But the sky appeared to wrap around the perimeter of where he was standing. Like if he started to run, he'd run in a big circle and end up right back where he had began. Like there was no way out. No place to go but forward.

Flip hopped up, onto his feet and dusted off the back of his jeans. He stepped up to the entrance of the maze and clenched his hands at his sides. They shook slightly with fear and anxiety of the unknown.

Before he stepped into the maze, Flip took a chance and called out. "Ms. Montgomery? Ro?!" He shouted out. "Are you there? Anybody?" He paused for a few beats and there was nothing. "Yep, it's official. I've lost my mind." Flip shook his head.

"Hello?!" A scared female voice shouted as if from an intercom system. The sound boomed from every direction.

"Ro?!" Flip called back.

A few moments later, "I hear you! Oh God, please help me!"

Flip's heart started to pound in his chest. "Where are you? Do you know where you are? Can you describe it to me?"

"I don't know! I'm in a room with no doors or windows. It's all wood with one couch and a chandelier above. That's it." Ro called back, panic choking her voice.

"It's okay, Ro. I'll find you, I swear." Flip reassured her.

"Are you the doctor that I've heard talking to Mary?" Ro asked.

"You heard us?" Flip asked in shock.

"I could hear everything. Who told you that there is a curse on my family? Did they tell you anything else? I don't know anything because everyone died before I could ask. I just know that everyone dies by the time they hit thirty." Ro asked in desperation.

"It was a gypsy. She told me that a woman put an ill wish on your family when your grandfather broke her heart." Flip told her as he pulled off his tank top and began ripping it into tiny shreds.

"Oh my God! Then it is true! How am I going to get out of this?" Ro asked. Flip could tell that she was on the verge of panic.

"It's alright, Ro. We'll figure this out together." Flip stepped gingerly into the maze and decided to go right. "I'm in a maze right now. I have no idea where it's going, but I will find you." Flip let her in on what was happening.

"Alright." Ro paused for a moment. "What's your name?"

Flip quickly walked down the first corridor, tied a strip of his shirt to the tall bush, and then turned left. "Dr. Flip Harris!" He shouted back to her.

"Did you say Flip, as in backflip?" Ro asked skeptically.

Flip chuckled and then made another right. "Yes Flip, as in backflip." He clarified.

"I-It's nice to m-meet you, Flip." Ro said in a wobbly voice.

"It's nice to meet you too, Ro. Don't freak out on me. Just breathe." Flip tried to soothe her.

"O-Okay." Ro replied.

"Alright. I might be kind of quiet while I try to figure out this maze. But don't worry, I'll still be here." Flip warned her.

"Thank you for doing this, Flip." Ro said sincerely.
"You're welcome."

Flip continued through the elaborate maze. He tied strips of cloth from his tank top at every turn to mark where he'd come from like bread crumbs. He was moving swiftly down one corridor and the wall of shrubs on either side of him started to close in on him. Flip started running as the walls got closer. His heart thumped in his chest and just as the walls slammed together, Flip dove forward, curling into a somersault as he rolled out of the way.

He looked back at where he'd come from and the entire maze had changed. "So much for my bread crumbs." Flip grumbled as he tossed away the rest of his torn tank.

"What was that?" Ro's voice called out.

"Oh, no worries. The maze just changed on me." Flip informed her.

Flip started to jog down the next corridor. This time he wasn't worried about where he'd come from. Now he was just worried about speed. He wanted to get through the maze as quickly as possible.

As he ran down a passageway, something tripped him and he fell hard. Flip tried to get up, but something was holding onto his leg. He looked back and a vine had wrapped itself around his ankle. Just then the vine started growing and more vines came out of the ground. They all started to wrap themselves around his body as he struggled.

Just when Flip thought it couldn't get any worse, he heard a hissing noise and looked down at his body to see that the vines had turned into snakes. They were everywhere. They were one of his biggest fears.

"Jesus!" Flip shouted out.

He started to dance around like a maniac, as he swiped and grabbed at the slithery creatures. Flip eventually freed himself and took off running down the passage to get as far from the snakes as quickly as possible.

"Flip, what happened?" Ro shouted.

"I'm okay. I just stumbled across my first test." He replied vaguely.

"Oh... Well, it didn't sound good." Ro said.

"It wasn't. Unless you like snakes." Flip tried to joke, though he was still shaken up.

"Oh God, no!" Ro gasped.

"Exactly. But don't worry, I'm alright." Flip assured her.

Flip continued running through the endless maze. He had been going for a while without a hitch and he started to think that maybe the snakes were his only test. He didn't think he really had anymore fears or phobias. He quickly found out how wrong he was.

He jogged around a turn in the maze and skidded to a halt. Standing before him was a small group of people. People that looked vaguely familiar. Then it hit him at the same time that one of them spoke.

"Why didn't you save me?" One of the men asked.

"Why did you let me die?" That was asked by a little girl.

The people who stood before him were past patients. Patients that died way before their time. Patients that he could not save.

Flip's knees buckled and he fell to the ground. His former patients crowded around him and he cowered in shame. All of them chanting the same things.

"I tried! I tried to save you!" Flip screamed at them as tears ran down his face. "There was nothing more that I could do," his voice cracked with pain.

"Flip, what's happening? Are you alright?" Ro's voice reached him through the den of haunted voices around him.

"They won't let me pass." Flip called out in anguish.

"Who?"

"My past patients. Patients that died because I wasn't good enough," Flip sobbed.

"Flip, don't say that. You're a brilliant surgeon and doctor. I heard the nurses talking about you." Ro encouraged. "They said that not only were you brilliant and saved so many lives, but that you're sweet and humble too. That you enjoy talking to your patients, getting to know them on a personal level."

"Yeah, I do. But it's not enough." Flip's large frame shook uncontrollably as he felt their cold hands on his curled up body.

"It has to be enough. You can't save everyone. But the fact that you try everything in your power to save them anyway, should be commended." Ro paused, letting her words sink in. "You're hear trying to save me, when you didn't have to. Don't let them destroy you. You have so many more lives that need you. So many more that you *will* save."

Flip felt strength from her words. He clenched his teeth and his jaw flexed tightly. He slowly stood up and their ghostly hands fell away.

"You let us die." They said, but their voices didn't carry the weight they first had.

"No, I didn't. I tried my best. I did everything I could. I'm sorry that you died, but some things, unfortunately, can't be fixed. You can't have me because there are more lives that I *can* save." Flip said with his head held high. "Now, let me pass."

The ghostly patients stepped aside and then faded away to nothing. Flip expelled a huge breath of relief and then took back in fortifying air.

"Thank you, Ro." Flip called out.

"No, thank you for going through this for me." Ro replied gratefully.

"Whatever it takes. I couldn't in good conscious, leave you here." Flip breathed as he continued through the maze.

"Are you riding up on a white horse too?" Ro tried to lighten the stressful mood.

"Nope. I left it parked outside." Flip grinned.

"So according to the nurses, you're pretty hot too." Ro commented.

"Ha! That's embarrassing." Flip shook his head.

"Well, technically it's only embarrassing if it isn't true. And I have a feeling that isn't the case." Ro's voice teased.

"Well...I guess you'll have to find out for yourself, when I find you." Flip teased back.

"I look forward to it." Flip heard the grin in her voice.

He continued on, though it started to feel like he was going in circles. Flip didn't feel any closer to the middle or end or wherever he was supposed to go, than when he'd first started the maze. He rounded another corner and again the green walls started to move. But this time, they started to close in on him from all sides.

"Shit!" He shouted as he looked for a way out, but not finding any.

"What? What is it?" Ro said anxiously.

"The walls are closing in on me, on all sides!" Flip started to panic.

The walls continued to close in on him and then suddenly stopped. Flip was left in a three by three foot square. He dropped down to his knees and looked up at the dark sky and grit his teeth in frustrated anger. He had no idea what to do because even if giving up was an option, he still had no idea how to get out himself.

"What's happening, Flip?" Ro asked impatiently.

"I'm trapped." Flip said, feeling like a failure.

"Oh..." Ro let the word hang in the air. "Well, you tried your best. It's more than I could've expected." She comforted.

"Was it?" Flip asked desolately.

Ro didn't respond, probably lost in her own thoughts. Flip sat down cross-legged on the grass carpeted ground. He heard the slight sounds of someone crying and he knew that it was Ro.

In every aspect of Flip's life, he had successfully jumped every hurdle he came across. He would approach each one as if it didn't exist. If one caused him difficulty and it was too high to jump over, he'd just barrel through it like a wrecking ball. There would be times that he'd fear failure and then he'd attack his fear like a rabid dog. This moment was no different. But this time there was someone waiting for him on the other side.

Flip took a deep breath. "Think, Flip. Think," he said to himself. "Wait a minute. Ro?!"

"Yes?" He heard her sniffle.

"The gypsy said that you were stuck in another dimension. That it wasn't the same as the regular world." Flip thought out loud.

"Yeah?" Ro asked not sure where he was going.

"Well, if this dimension can change depending on one's fears, doesn't it stand to reason that it could change considering one's strengths too?" He asked.

"Maybe…" Ro said softly, as if she didn't want to get too excited.

Flip began to imagine jumping this hurdle and the moment he did the ground started to move up.

"Ro! The ground is moving! It's moving up!" Flip shouted out with excitement.

"And that's a good thing?!" Ro asked hesitantly.

"Yes!" Flip grinned as the floor continued up like an elevator.

Eventually the floor rose up high enough that the shrubs only reached hip level on Flip. In the middle of the maze, he could see a small cottage with no windows or doors. He instantly began to run through the maze, finding his way easily.

"I think I found you!" Flip bellowed as he neared the cottage.

"Really?! Oh, thank God!" Ro breathed in relief.

Flip reached the cottage and quickly jogged around the perimeter to see if he could find any opening. There weren't any. He growled in frustration and rested his hands and forehead against the wall of the cottage.

"Ro?" Flip called softly.

"Yeah?"

"There aren't any doors or windows on the outside either." He paused and she didn't respond. "Maybe now it's time to face your fears." Flip suggested.

"This is my fear." Ro said softly. "This curse has hovered over my head since I was a little girl. I lived in fear that I would die at any time, any day. I've tried to live a perfect life in the hopes that that would release me from the curse. Nothing worked and now I'm living my greatest nightmare." Ro's voice wobbled.

"I'm so sorry, Ro." Flip whispered against the wall.

"It's not your fault, Flip. And you know what?" Ro said, her voice gaining strength.

"What?"

"It's not my fault either. I am not my grandfather and I shouldn't have to pay for his deeds." Ro said angrily.

Flip flinched away from the wall, when before his eyes a door started to slowly materialize.

"Ro! Keep going! A door is forming! Keep going!" Flip shouted.

"I am not my grandfather! I am sorry for what he did to you. I'm sorry he broke your heart, but our family has paid the price. We've paid enough. I'm not him, I would never turn my back on love." Ro said loudly and firmly.

The door finally solidified in front of Flip and he slowly reached for the door as if it would disappear any second. His fingers touched the doorknob, but it didn't vanish. He wrapped his fingers around it and turned the knob. There was a satisfying click and Flip pushed the door open. On the other side stood the most beautiful sight he could've imagined.

~~~

The door swung open and Ro inhaled sharply at the sight that greeted her. Flip was the most gorgeous man she had ever seen. And to top it off, he had saved her…twice. The man had stopped at nothing to bring her back.

Ro wasn't sure what it was that propelled her straight into his arms; maybe gratitude, relief, or even love. All she knew is one second she was staring at the handsome man and next she was in his strong arms.

Flip held onto her tightly, his hand cupping the back of her head as she buried her face in his chest. After a while, Ro pulled back slightly to look up at him. Flip brushed her blonde locks back and he took her face between his large hands. Her hazel eyes looked up honestly, into his warm brown eyes.

"Hello." Flip said deeply.

"Hi." Ro smiled shyly.

Flip crushed his lips to hers and she opened up to him without question. When they broke apart and opened their eyes, they were safe and sound in Flips master bedroom on his king size bed.

"We're back! You saved my life." Ro said in wonder as she gently touched her fingers to his square jaw.

"And I'd do it again everyday if I had to, just to be near you." Flip said sincerely.

Ro's eyes filled with tears and she closed the space between them. She kissed him softly and Flip groaned as he pulled her towards him. She flicked her tongue against his, giving him the okay to take it further. Flip held her tightly and Ro could feel his arousal against her stomach. She lifted her leg to rest on his hip, bringing his erection flush against her seeking heat through her hospital gown. Flip released her lips, his breath came hot and hard as he searched her face.

"Are you sure? Are you up for this? I don't want to hurt you." Flip asked considerately, thinking she'd had surgery not that long ago.

"Yes, I'm sure. I've never been so sure of anything in my life. All my life, I've played it safe. I want to be reckless. And with you." Ro ended on a kiss and a playful nip to his bottom lip.

"Yes, ma'am." Flip grinned before devouring her mouth.

Ro rolled up onto Flip and she straddled his hips. He reached behind her and pulled the ties of her hospital gown. The gown slid down her naked body and Flip looked up at her soft and stunning body. Her large, creamy breasts were heavy and tipped a pale brown. Her waist was thick and tummy soft. Ro hips flared slightly and extended to her pliable, fleshy thighs that cushioned his waist and hips. Her fair sun-kissed skin, flush against his honeyed tone was a striking contrast.

Ro raised her hips and unzipped his jeans, releasing his thick, stiff length. Flip helped her shimmy his pants and boxers down his legs. She clasped him in her small warm hands, positioning him at her slick entrance. She slowly sunk down on his pretty cock and he stretched her to capacity. Ro threw her head back as she reached the base of his manhood.

Flip growled deep in his throat at the feeling of her wrapped tightly around him. It had been a year since he'd made love to a woman, and he felt his scrotum already drawing up. He clenched his teeth together to hold back. He pumped up into her wet cleft as he held her hips in place. He was ready to explode at any second and he knew she wasn't ready yet.

He flipped her over and swiftly pulled out of her torturously tight warmth. He quickly bent down and licked up her wet crease and Ro bucked against his mouth. Flips tongue caressed her pink labia, teasing her. He finally latched onto her swollen clit and suckled gently. Ro cried out to the room and he continued to lap at her sweet nectar. She quickly came apart and Flip hastily sat up and drove into her flexing channel, while she was still in the middle of an amazing orgasm.

    Flip rested his forehead against Ro's and he looked into her eyes, their breath mingling harshly between them as he continued to pump into her. His tongue flicked at her open mouth and her tongue caressed his back. Her inner walls still rippled around him.

    "Fuck, Ro! I can't hold back. Give me another. Just one more." Flip panted.

    Ro's body tensed and released on a scream as she dissolved into the throes of another intense climax. Flip felt her release crest over him and he finally let go. Her muscles milked him and he moaned deeply.

    "Stay." Flip panted against her lips.

    "Where else would I go?" Ro replied breathlessly.

    Two matching smiles spread across their faces and a happy giggle escaped Ro's lips. Joy spread throughout her chest. The curse had been a dark cloud over her head for so long, she never dreamed that it would be a blessing in disguise. And as she looked up at Flip's gorgeous smile, she realized that no matter what, the sun would always rise to light up the darkness.

••••

白雪姫
Yuki Shiro

Kyoto, Japan 1854

    *P*rincess Yuki walked the gardens of the Imperial Palace, humming softly. She tossed out food for the koi fish swimming in the ponds. As soon as they saw her above the water, they swam over, waiting impatiently for her to feed them.

    "So greedy." Yuki scolded the fish. "If only I were a fish, then I could be as greedy as you. And no one would have to worry about finding a man that's willing to marry the fat princess. The disappointment of Japan." Yuki said resentfully. She tugged at her tight obi that wrapped around her waist, holding her kimono together and forcing her thick waist inward.

    When the princess was born, her pale skin reminded her father, the Emperor of Japan, of the pure white snow after a heavy snowfall. The Emperor fondly named her Yuki Shiro, *Snow White*. After her mother passed away, the Emperor doted on his only child. Giving her whatever she asked for; toys, ponies, sweets, etc. In the end the beautiful princess became soft and curvy from overindulging.

    A full-figure in her culture wasn't found attractive. Slender, delicate frames with little to no curves were the standards of beauty. So once she grew to a marriageable age, no man was interested. People of the aristocracy often told her that it was a shame, since she had such a beautiful face.

    Which was why Yuki preferred to spend her time alone in the palace gardens. The birds, fish, and other animals that came to visit her, couldn't speak or criticize her. And instead of focusing on how to look pretty with makeup and clothing, Yuki focused on the Arts. As well as passing out food and spending time with the commoners near the palace. As a result she was an expert musician. She loved to sing and play the biwa and shakuhachi, a Japanese guitar and flute. And she was well loved by her community.

Though even with all her extra-curricular activities, Yuki's melancholy only increased when her father married Kasumi, a very beautiful but domineering and cruel woman. She treated Yuki like a second class citizen and looked at her with unconcealed disgust. And Yuki was not fooled when her father suddenly became ill, shortly after the wedding.

He father was still holding on, but just barely. Yuki knew that Kasumi was somehow responsible for keeping him sick. Though, she had no way to prove it. She knew that even as the princess, she better have more proof than a hunch, before accusing the Empress of foul play.

Yuki sighed deeply as she tried to shake off her dejected mood. She kneeled down at the edge of the pond and ran her fingers lightly over the crystal clear surface of the water. The large fish nibbled happily on her fingers, tickling her fingertips. Yuki giggled, her chortle sounding more like music than laughter.

"Yuki! Stop cackling and cavorting with those stupid fish and come inside to help with the feast for tonight." Kasumi shouted angrily from the doorway.

"Yes, Empress." Yuki submitted and quickly walked inside under the watchful glare of her stepmother.

~~~

That night, the palace held a large gathering inside a huge tent on the elaborate palace grounds. It was in honor of the trade agreement Japan made with America. There were several Japanese dignitaries and noblemen in attendance. Some were in traditional Japanese garb and others opting for western style formal suits. The American men wore their tailored suits and military uniforms to perfection. Atop their heads were bowlers and top hats in black, gray, brown and tan.

One American man in particular, Yuki's eyes immediately gravitated towards. Something about him seemed a little wild and untamed. Many of the Americans wore white wigs or powder in their natural hair, but this man's long raven colored hair was untouched. He wore it pulled back with a brown leather tie at the nape of his neck. Most of the men were clean shaven or had fancy mustaches, where his face was covered in a light, jet-black beard.

He wore a black double-breasted short coat with tails, a white waistcoat underneath, and pristine white pantaloons that scandalously showed off his powerful thighs. Black knee-high riding boots graced his feet, and a white cravat around his neck. Though his ensemble was just as formal as the other men at the fancy dinner, his powerful body under the clothes and his sharp silver gaze, hinted to the feral heart under the surface. Yuki was entranced.

She was not alone. The American, Yuki had been watching, Cade McAllister, had eyes only for her. His silvery gaze landed on the stunning princess the moment he walked through the open entrance of the large tent. She greeted the guests with a deep bow at the waist and downcast eyes, refusing to make eye contact.

The princess wore a deep red kimono with cherry blossom details embroidered around the sleeves and hemline. A white obi cinched in her waist and held the kimono together. Her ebony hair wasn't as elaborate as the other women's. Hers was pulled up into a high intricate bun with silk cherry blossoms that hung from the side of it and trembled with her every breath. And unlike the other Japanese women in attendance the princess had foregone the white makeup on her face, since it appeared that her skin was already the palest shade of white. She only wore rouge on her Cupid's bow lips in the deepest of reds. And kohl on her sultry hooded eyes to emphasize their beauty.

They both tried to keep their attraction hidden. For Yuki, it would be inappropriate to stare at a man. And Cade didn't want to disrespect the Empress by staring down her stepdaughter.

Everyone sat at a long western style banquet table to accommodate the Americans in attendance. During their dealings with westerners before, the palace knew that not everyone was comfortable sitting on the floor to eat if they weren't used to it.

Cade sat several chairs down from the Empress and princess during the elaborate dinner, in a position of lesser importance. After all, he was just a lowly merchant and expert huntsman. He had spent many hours hunting with Japan's finest dignitaries and trading their wares. So Cade had gained a good reputation, which was why he was invited to the grand feast.

Though during his time in Japan, Cade had yet to meet the princess until this night. None of the men he had spent time with ever talked about her, so he knew nothing about the beautiful woman. He planned on changing that later, if he got the chance.

Yuki surreptitiously watched Cade out the corner of her eye. She wondered what his story was. Though, she knew that it didn't matter. The country would rather see her become a spinster than to be with a foreigner. She sighed heavily at the tragedy of her current and future love life.

Yuki's woolgathering was interrupted by a solid looking General with a blond curling mustache, sitting across from her. "How long has the Emperor been sick, Princess?"

"Hmm…just about as long as my father has been married to Empress Kasumi." Yuki said boldly before turning to her stepmother and raising a finely arched black brow. "Isn't that right Empress?"

"Yes, some terrible unknown disease befell my dear husband not long after our marriage began." The Empress said to the General and then looked to Yuki barely concealing a chilling glare. "I'm surprised you even noticed, Yuki. I mean, with your face buried in sweets and talking to animals all day, I'm amazed you've had time to pay attention to anything else."

Yuki was mortified by the insult. The other Japanese noblemen at the table chuckled at the joke. Though the Americans seemed clueless as to what was so funny. Yuki quickly got up and excused herself. She knew that she had probably made a dire mistake by calling out the Empress and bringing to her attention the fact that Yuki was accusing her of foul play. But she was just so fed up with the Empress and her cruelty.

Yuki fled the large tent and ran towards her personal garden. Tears streamed down her face as she collapsed in front of her favorite pond filled with her beloved koi fish. The full moon was reflected in the still surface of the water. A single tear fell into the water, causing ripples in the serene reflection.

"Princess? Are you alright?" A deep voice startled Yuki.

She quickly wiped at her tear-streaked face before turning to address the interloper. "I'm fine." Yuki turned to see the handsome dark haired American she had been fascinated with all evening.

"You don't seem fine. Do you want to talk about it?" He coaxed.

"I don't think it's proper for you to be talking to me in a dark garden without a suitable chaperone." Yuki warned.

"Well, I don't know about you, Princess. But I like a little danger and excitement in my life. Keeps the blood circulating," he said with a devilish smile. "I'm Cade

McAllister, by the way." He introduced himself with an extended hand to shake.

Yuki looked at his large, rough hand for a few seconds. She knew it was improper to be alone with this strange man. It was also their custom to bow instead of shake hands, but her pale, delicate hand reached out towards the fire and clasped his hand anyway. Cade's massive paw wrapped around the fragile bones of her hand and shook gently. A thrill shot up Yuki's arm and radiated down her body. A small gasp escaped her lips.

"Yuki Shiro. Though you can call me Yuki." She greeted him as he still held onto her hand.

"What does your name mean, Yuki?" Cade asked curiously.

"Snow white."

"Hmm…it suits you." He noted as he looked at her skin that was nearly translucent in the moonlight.

"Thank you," she said demurely, feeling bashful.

Yuki tried to pull her hand free of his, but Cade had other plans. His hand tightened and he pulled her up onto her feet. She lost her balance and collided with his wide chest. Cade steadied her with his hands on her soft shoulders. She looked up at him with sad dark brown eyes.

"Now, what was so terrible about what the Empress said to you?" Cade asked.

Yuki flushed in embarrassment, realizing that he had overheard the insult. "I…I'm not considered…attractive," was all that she could get out. She then turned her head in shame.

"What are you talking about?" Cade asked bewildered. "You're gorgeous!

"I'm fat. Which is why I'm still unmarried. I'm told that no man wants a fat wife." Yuki said looking down at the ground.

Cade placed his fingers under her chin and lifted her face up to his. "I'm not sure what the requirements are for beauty here, but where I come from you are stunning. A woman that is strong enough to work alongside her husband during the day, in a sometimes unforgiving country." Cade lifted the hand on her chin to stroke down her soft cheek. "Yet, soft and pliant enough to tempt a man to his bed at night, and never want to leave. That's a woman a man wants, where I'm from."

Cade's words and silver gaze nearly buckled Yuki's knees. No one had ever dared to speak to her so frankly before. No one had ever looked at her with desire either. She had never found anyone that she thought was desirable, for that matter. So the heat that pulsed through her veins. The butterflies that stirred up a commotion in her tummy. And the pool of moisture that gathered at the apex of her legs that made her squirm, were all feelings that were completely new to her.

The desperate need in her to feel wanted, to feel affection, overrode her need for propriety. So as Cade's sculpted lips descended to hers, Yuki opened up to him like a lotus flower. The silk cherry blossoms that adorned her hair quivered as her body trembled with barely contained desire.

Cade traced her bottom lip with his tongue and she opened for him on a sharp intake of air. Once she let him in, he drank from her lips and tongue thirstily. The princess timidly touched her tongue to his, trying to imitate him and Cade's control slipped slightly. A growled rumbled through him and he deepened the kiss, devouring her sweet mouth and abrading her soft skin with his beard.

The quick flicks and soft caresses of his warm, wet tongue made the arousal that had pooled at the entrance of her sex, drip down her inner thigh. Yuki squeezed her thighs together in an attempt to stop the flow, as well as the throbbing that had begun in her most secret of places. Cade had just wrapped his arms firmly around her and she had gotten a hint of his solid arousal, when a voice broke the spell.

"Princess? Are you here?" The voice of Yuki's trusted maid Mai, called out in concern.

Cade reluctantly pulled away from the princess and melted into the darkness of the garden as Mai walked further into the garden. Yuki felt chilled after the warmth of his embrace, and she wrapped her arms around herself.

"I'm here, Mai." Yuki spoke up, her voice sounding shaky to her own ears.

"Oh, thank goodness! I was worried when I didn't see you in the tent." Mai smiled sweetly at her.

"I'm fine. But I think I'll retire now. I'm no longer in the mood to socialize." Yuki admitted.

"Yes, Princess. I'll take you to your room and help you dress for bed." Mai said, taking Yuki's arm gently.

"Thank you, Mai." Yuki said and then looked back to where Cade had disappeared into the night. Though she saw nothing.

Cade was an expert at blending into his surroundings. He knew she couldn't see him, but he watched Yuki turn and walk into the palace. His heart still pounded in his chest and his erection strained against the soft cotton of his pantaloons. He took a moment to compose himself before rejoining the festivities. Though it was harder than he thought, due to the memory of her small sweet mouth and warm soft curves against him.

He had no idea when or how he'd see the princess again, but Cade vowed to make it happen as he strode back towards the tent.

Later that night Yuki dreamed of Cade. In her dream, he touched and kissed her everywhere. He brought her to the brink of something unknown to her and she awoke abruptly. Her skin was covered in a light sheen of perspiration. Her heart rate accelerated and her pulse pounded, but she didn't feel it in her veins. She felt it at her now soaked, forbidden garden.

Yuki didn't dare touch herself there, so she squeezed her legs together tightly, hoping to stop the aching throb. The pressure only made it worse and she quickly jumped out of bed in frustration. Yuki felt a restlessness that she had never experienced before. She paced around her bedroom for a while and when that didn't help, she decided that a walk down to the gardens would soothe her ache, like it always did when she was in turmoil.

As she padded barefoot through the palace, Yuki heard something peculiar. She followed the noise. She realized it was a conversation, but one side of it sounded garbled, like it was coming from underwater. She also recognized Empress Kasumi's voice. The conversation was coming from her stepmother's private garden.

Yuki snuck in through Kasumi's bedroom to the doorway into the garden. She peeked her head around and had to clasp her hand over her mouth to cover the gasp that came from her lips. The princess blinked several times in the hopes that she was just imagining things. But every time she opened her eyes, she saw the same image.

Kasumi was standing in front of her own private pond and before her rising out of the water was a figure. The figure was made of glowing blue, rippling water that was formed into Kasumi's doppelgänger. Yuki stood rooted to the spot in shock. Then finally, the conversation between the Empress and the watery apparition sunk into Yuki's consciousness.

"Yurei, today I heard the Americans praise the beauty of the princess. Am I not still the most beautiful woman of this land?" Kasumi asked the apparition.

"No Empress, you are not. Princess Yuki embodies beauty from within that radiates throughout. The people of this land revere and respect her. They fear and loathe you because they believe you have kept their beloved Emperor sick. The princess suspects you as well." The garbled voice of the watery ghost warned Kasumi.

"I must get rid of that simpering brat, before she ruins everything! Yurei, please tell me how I can destroy her for good?" The Empress pleaded.

"You must take her heart. If you do the people of this land will only see her beautiful spirit when they see you. Then they will revere you as you wish. Power will be yours." The spirit advised her.

Yuki's heart nearly pounded out of her chest in fear at hearing the plans for her demise. Before she could be caught, she quietly slipped back out into the hallway. She then ran full speed to her rooms. Yuki quickly dressed in one of her plainer kimonos and grabbed a small pouch filled with money. She slipped out of her room and heard footsteps making their way towards her from down the hall. Her heart nearly exploded as she ran on bare feet towards her maid's room. She tiptoed into the sparse room and shook her trusted maid awake.

"Mai, please wake up." Yuki begged quietly.

"What is it, Princess?" Mai asked groggily.

"I can't explain right now, but I need your help to escape the palace!" Yuki said as she pulled a sleepy Mai out of bed.

Yuki threw articles of clothing to Mai and in a complete role reversal, she helped her maid into her clothes.

"Princess, this is highly inappropriate." Mai said as Yuki tied her obi around her kimono.

"It's okay, Mai. There's no time to waste." Yuki hushed the self-conscious servant.

Once Mai was fully dressed they ran to the palace stables.

"Alright, Mai. I just overheard the Empress plotting to kill me. To take my heart! And with a spirit! I must go into hiding and figure out a way to expose her for what she really is." Yuki explained in a frightened whisper.

Mai's mouth flapped opened and closed in response.

"I remember that you told me once, many of your family still live in the mountains. Living the way of the Samurai. Do you think they could protect me?" Yuki asked desperately.

"Yes, I think so." Mai finally found her tongue.

"Do you think you could take me there? Do you remember where to go?" Yuki asked anxiously.

"Yes, Princess. I remember." Mai nodded.

"Perfect. Okay, we must go now." Yuki said stepping into the stall of one of the horses.

The women quickly prepared two horses for their long journey. Yuki tried to keep the fear of being killed, in the forefront of her mind to combat her fear of leaving the palace and surrounding village. She had never venture far from the familiar surroundings of the Imperial Palace and village, and never without an entourage of guards or escorts. But she didn't find the idea of getting her heart ripped out, appealing in the least. So she set aside her trepidation and mounted her horse and kicked at his sides, starting him out at a soft canter as to not alert the entire palace of her escape. Mai followed closely behind.

As they approached the high gate and guards keeping sentry, Yuki raised the hood to her dark cloak over her head, slumped forward, and started moaning as if in pain. Mai took the lead so that she could speak to the guards.

"Why are you about so late, Mai?" One of the guards spoke.

"One of the servant girls has become ill. We think it may be cholera." Mai said to the man she knew had a fondness for her.

Both guards took a step back in fear and one quickly opened the gate for the women to slip through.

"Be well, Mai." He said fearful for himself and Mai, hoping an outbreak didn't spread throughout the palace.

Yuki breathed a sigh of relief as she and Mai made their way into the night, disappearing in the forebodingly thick fog.

~~~

"Empress?" A servant said timidly, afraid of the woman's wrath.

"What?!" Kasumi bellowed. She had been furious when she'd found Yuki's room empty, as if the girl had disappeared into thin air. Her mood had not improved each passing minute the princess was not found.

The Empress had had the servants check the palace from top to bottom. When the princess had not materialized, she then told them to discreetly search the village. She didn't want the villagers or anyone else for that matter to know that the princess had disappeared. If all else failed, she could send someone out to find and kill her, bringing back her heart and no one would be the wiser.

"The huntsman is here to see you." The servant bowed low averting his eyes.

"Well what are you waiting for?! Send him in!" Kasumi screeched.

"Yes, your Highness." The man bowed repetitiously as he back out of the room.

Kasumi watched as the tall, broad, dark-haired American walked into the room. She noted that he looked confident, lethal. Just what she needed. She also needed an outsider, none of the inhabitants of Japan would do what she requested because of their loyalty to the princess.

"Huntsman, I need to request your services." Kasumi sat up straighter on her throne.

"What do you ask of me, Empress? I would be honored to assist you in whatever you need." The huntsman offered gallantly.

"This job requires discretion. I want no one to know of what I ask. Do you swear to hold your tongue, else I remove it?" Kasumi asked firmly, looking the man straight in the eye, unblinking.

"Yes, your Highness," he said inclining his head.

"Good. The princess has disappeared. I need you to find her." Kasumi informed him.

"Of course, Empress. That's simple enough."

"When you find her, kill her. And bring back her heart." The Empress's cold voice rang out, surprising the man. "Is this something you can do, huntsman? Or do I need to find someone else?" *And then execute you before you speak a word of this?* She thought in her head.

"No, Empress. It is no problem. I will leave as soon as I can ready my horse." The huntsman assured her.

"Perfect." Kasumi grabbed a medium sized box to hand to the huntsman. "Place her heart in this box and bring it back to me. Now go and don't return until the deed has been completed." She finished, dismissing him.

~~~

Cade loaded his horse with some supplies for his journey. He looked down at the elaborate box in his hand. It was stained in a shiny black lacquer with a beautiful golden tree painted on it and red Japanese characters. The box would've been stunning to him, if it wasn't for its sinister purpose.

He breathed a silent sigh of relief that he was the man the Empress had requested to find Yuki. Had it been anyone else, Yuki would surely be heading to her death. Cade had no intentions of killing the princess, only protecting her.

Cade placed the box in his saddlebag. He planned to smash the offensive box and toss it into a passing river the moment he was a safe distance away. He had been filled with anxious excitement when he'd been summoned to the palace, in the hopes of seeing Yuki again. Never could he have imagined the evil plan being weaved at the hands of the Empress.

Though, Cade was pleased that he was off to a good start in finding the princess. One of the guards at the Imperial Palace told him that the princess's favorite maid had left with another woman on horseback two nights prior. Cade had thanked God that it hadn't rained when he found the faint hoof prints of two horses heading in the direction of the mountains.

Soon, Princess.

They slowly made their way up another steep incline that Mai claimed would be the last before they reached the village, though Yuki wasn't so sure. Her maid had said that about the last three inclines.

Just then, the foliage on either side of the road rustled slightly and two rather serious looking men jumped out onto the path in front of them. Their thin, sharp samurai swords drawn.

"Who goes there?" One shouted out.

"It's Mai, cousin to Masaru. We're here to speak to your leader, Takashi." Mai called out to the men. Surprise written on their faces at hearing their leader's name.

"Little Mai?" One man asked in shock, a happy grin spread across his face. Apparently, he remembered Mai as a little girl.

"Yes."

"Who's with you?" The other man asked still wary, a grumpy scowl marring his face.

Mai sat up a little straighter in her saddle. "Princess Yuki."

The men immediately burst out into skeptical laughter.

"Sure, Mai. And I'm the Emperor!" The silly looking man joked.

Yuki clasped the hood of her cape, pushed it back and let it drop to her shoulders. The laughter died in the men's throats. Images of the princess in embroidery and paintings had been spread across the country. So the men knew what she looked like.

"Oh, Princess! Please forgive us!" The serious one apologized as they both bowed repeatedly.

"It's alright. What are your names?" Yuki said graciously.

"I'm Kenji." The silly one spoke first.

"And I'm Ren," said the serious one.

"Hello, gentlemen. I'm pleased to meet you." Yuki inclined her head politely.

"Please Princess, let us escort you the rest of the way to the village." Ren stepped forward and took the reins of Yuki's horse.

"Yes, we'll take you to Takashi." Kenji happily took Mai's reins from her to lead her horse as well.

Half an hour later, they rounded a corner on the mountain, and an adorably quaint village came into view. Several men and women were working outside. Some were working in the fields tending their crops, some men were chopping wood or fixing roofs.

Many of the men were sparring out in the grass. One set were working on their wrestling skills. Another group were shooting arrows into far off targets. And the last cluster were lunging at each other with wooden swords.

As the four made their way into the middle of the village, all the activity died down as the villagers looked up curiously. Once they noticed the regal posture of the princess and looked up to see her face, their mouths fell open in shock as recognition hit. They all bowed in deference.

Ren and Kenji helped Yuki and Mai down from their horses. Meanwhile, their village leader, Takashi and four other men that had been working on their swordplay, walked forward to greet their new guests. Yuki noticed that the leader's eyes continually landed on her maid. They were filled with attraction and affection, before they finally landed on her, ready for introductions.

"Princess. I am Takashi. Leader of this village." Takashi bowed deeply. "I am honored to welcome you to our village."

"Thank you, Takashi." Yuki bowed in return. "I must admit that I am here because I need your help," she confessed.

"Please Princess, walk with me and we shall talk. I will introduce you to the village later." Takashi held out his hand gesturing for Yuki to follow him.

Yuki walked along beside the respected man as she explained what had become of her father after his marriage five years ago. She also told him of what she saw a few nights before and the Empress's plan to kill her. Takashi vowed to protect her and quickly introduced her to his strongest, bravest samurai warriors.

"Princess, myself and my six best men will protect you with our lives." Takashi walked her back over to the group of men and Mai. "You've already met Kenji and Ren."

"Yes, and thanks again, to both of you for bringing us the rest of the way safely." Yuki said kindly as they both bowed.

"The rest are Yoshi, Nobu, Shin and Masaru." Takashi pointed to each one he introduced and they bowed in turn. "If you need anything, we will be more than happy to assist you. For now you and Mai will stay in my home, since it is the biggest. At least until we can come up with a plan to remove the Empress from her position of power."

"Thank you, Takashi. I don't know how to repay you," Yuki said.

"Having a princess in my home is payment enough. The village will speak about this for centuries to come." Takashi smiled proudly.

Takashi led them to his house. He opened the paper screen and gestured inside. He quickly got them settled into individual rooms and fed them lunch. Yuki watched as Takashi pressed his suit for Mai and how her pretty maid responded shyly but happily.

Yuki sighed wistfully, wishing that she could find someone that wanted her at first glance. Suddenly, dark hair and gray eyes clouded her vision and a warmth spread through her veins, tingles prickled her skin, and moisture dampened her thighs. Her mood immediately worsened, knowing that she would probably never see the rugged American again.

~~~

The princess woke up again covered in sweat. Ever since she had met Cade, her dreams had been filled with entwined limbs, gentle caresses and soft lips. And as always, she woke up flustered and frustrated.

    Yuki pushed herself up from her soft pallet, slightly disoriented. After lunch and a quick tour of the village the day before, she had been exhausted from their long journey and went to lie down. When she woke up after her nap, the villagers had prepared a great feast in celebration of the princess being in their village. After the meal the seven samurais put on a silly play, making Yuki and the villagers laugh happily.

    The princess had felt completely at ease and like one of the villagers, as she enjoyed the festivities. They didn't look down on her, like the nobility did for her weight. And they'd treated her more like one of their own. Unlike the villagers near the palace that treated her reverently because of her station. So she enjoyed feeling like a part of something, after being lonely for so long.

    They'd passed around sake and Yuki had developed at fuzzy haze that had made her relax further. Which was when the silly one, Kenji, had pulled her up to dance. Eventually, Yuki had done a solo performance with fans, to the delight of the villagers.

    Once she had finished, she was completely drained. So Mai helped her to her room and that was the last she remembered. From the light coming in through the window, Yuki could tell it was just before dawn.

    She hadn't had a proper bath in days and she felt disgusting. Yuki looked around the room and spotted a bundle of plain clothing next to the door. She quickly got up and grabbed the kimono and obi. Takashi had shown them where the hot springs were located for bathing and she had every intention of enjoying a hot bath in private.

    Yuki quietly tiptoed out of her new bedroom and down the hall. She heard a rhythmic thumping and the sounds of moaning coming from Mai's room. Worried, Yuki quickly walked over to her door and slid the door open a crack to check on her maid. The sight that greeted her, shocked and aroused her instantly.

Takashi was in between Mai's legs and his buttocks flexed as he pumped towards her. Their naked limbs tangled together passionately. Yuki quickly closed the door and stumbled back towards the door leading outside. Flushed with embarrassment, she quickly made her way in the pale light of dawn to the hot spring.

Steam rose up from the still water in the cool autumn air. Yuki toed off her wooden sandals and let her dirty, smudged kimono she'd arrived in, slide off her shoulders and fall to the stone floor. She untied her undershirt and skirt, they too met with the kimono on the ground.

The chill in the air rose the gooseflesh on Yuki's skin and beaded her pale brown nipples. She stepped down quickly into the hot water, trying to escape the cold air. Once she was enveloped in the warmth of the water, Yuki raised her hands to her hair. She released her hair from the pins holding it up in a bun and relieved the pain in her scalp. Her hair cascaded down around her and its inky blackness floated around her in the water. She took a deep breath and sunk down, letting the water swallow her whole.

~~~

Cade stood mesmerized as he watched Yuki in the hot spring. Just before dawn he had followed the hoof prints to the perimeter of the little village. He knew there were guards stationed just out of sight of the road. So Cade led his horse into the forest and tied off it near a pond. He circled around through the woods to see if there were any signs that the princess had sought refuge there. He had no idea what he would find at the hot springs that took up residence just at the forest's edge.

He had intended to step out from behind the thick foliage to make his presence known, when Yuki first walked to the pool of hot water. But she hadn't wasted anytime in stripping down and stepping in the water. So he stood rooted to the spot as she bared herself to the woods. To him.

Her body made him want to weep with need. The women in Japan were beautiful, though the majority were slender and small. Their shape hidden behind layers of formal clothing. Seeing Yuki's thick inward curving waist, flared hips, soft thighs, and full brown-tipped breasts was like a starving man seeing a grand feast for the first time. Cade realized that he was starving.

Yuki ducked her head under the water and Cade stepped out of the greenery that was hiding him. He stood at the edge of the springs, waiting for her to rise. When she finally did, her back was to him. She slowly turned around as she pushed back the hair from her face. Droplets of water clung to her pale skin, dusky brown nipples, and spiky black lashes.

The princess opened her eyes and swallowed down a scream when she realized she was not alone. Her eyes swiftly looked up from the brown boots at her eye level to the handsome visage above. A face that had been haunting her dreams for days.

Yuki wrapped her arms around her bare breasts. Cade's silver gaze felt like it went right through her and hardened her nipples to tiny pebbles. She bent her knees to submerge her body to her shoulders, trying her best to cover her naked body.

"Yuki." Cade whispered her name sensually. "I'm sorry for scaring you. I've tracked you for days and I wasn't expecting you to be taking a dip in the springs.

"W-Why are you tracking me?" Yuki asked shyly.

Cade bent over and pulled off his boots and rolled up the brown pant legs of his trousers. He sat down on the rock ledge and placed his feet in the hot water before continuing.

"The Empress sent me," he said seriously.

Yuki instantly backed away in fear.

"I would never hurt you, Princess." Cade looked at her sincerely. "She asked me to bring back your heart. And I am so glad that she sent me to do it because if it had of been anyone else, you'd be dead. I'm here to protect you, Yuki. I would die before I let her touch a hair on your head." Cade vowed passionately.

Yuki studied his handsome face for several minutes. She searched for dishonesty there and found none. As she stared at him and realized he was staring right back, Yuki became hyperaware of her nakedness under the water. She also recalled the passionate lovemaking between Takashi and Mai and her pulse immediately sped up. Her breath hitched in her throat and she shivered despite the heat of the water surrounding her.

Cade saw the arousal written all over Yuki's face and he went out on a limb. He was going to ask if she minded if he joined her, but he had a feeling that she would reject him for propriety's sake. So instead he stood back up and slowly started to remove his clothing.

Yuki's dark chestnut eyes widened with a mix of excitement and fear. She knew that she should turn around to give him privacy, but she was frozen in place. Her eyes glued to his large frame.

Cade shrugged off his long navy blue jacket and unbuttoned his calf brown vest. He pulled his off-white, leather lace-front shirt over his head. In the process, he revealed broad shoulders, defined pectorals, and sculpted abdominals.

The princess knew she should tell him to stop. That he couldn't come in with her, but her curiosity. Her need to feel wanted and her desire to feel what Mai had felt, when she'd peeked into her room earlier. All overrode her need to say no.

Yuki breathed in deeply when Cade boldly unsnapped his trousers and pulled them and his underpants down. They fell to his ankles and the breath she didn't know she was holding, exploded between her lips at the sight of his jutting erection. Yuki had never seen a fully naked man, especially not his most private area. It was beautiful, scary, and foreign to her. Yet her hidden place, between her legs flexed involuntarily at the sight of him.

Cade saw the fear and excitement in her eyes as he stepped down into the steaming pool. If she'd have said no, he would've stopped, but she said nothing. So he answered his body's call to get inside her, to please her and moved towards her till he was only inches away.

"You can say no, Yuki," he said. *But please don't!* He thought to himself.

"Please." She said instead. Unable to say yes or no. Yuki could only plead with him to help her stop the ache that had been gnawing at her since she'd met him.

Cade clasped her face with both hands and wasted little time in descending for a heated kiss. He ravaged her lips, like that starving man finally getting a taste of the feast before him. Yuki's arms that had been covering her breasts were now smashed between them. She wriggled them free and clutched his strong biceps, trying her best to hold on and finally closing the few inches left between them. Now their bodies were completely aligned.

The feeling of her nipples against the slight fur of his chest, made them hardened further. The coarse hair on his muscular thighs abraded the soft skin of hers. And the smooth hardness of his erection, rested against her pubic bone and soft tummy. The contrasts thrilled Yuki and she soon forgot about her shyness.

Cade had little control over his hips as he pumped forward, sliding his hard cock against her soft tummy, the slick warm water adding him. He was desperate to get inside her, but he knew that she was a virgin and didn't deserve a rutting bastard to take it callously.

So he released her lips and he placed soft kisses over her face, leaving no feature untouched. Cade kissed down her jawline to her smooth neck, and then soft shoulder. He slowly made his way around to her back and caressed his lips across the top, shoulder to shoulder. Cade came back around to her front and the look in her heavy-lidded eyes told him that she was just as on fire as he. He reached down and gripped her ass, lifting Yuki off of her feet. He walked her to the edge of the pool and hoisted her up to sit on the edge.

Yuki's full breasts and brown tipped peaks were at the perfect, mouthwatering level. She watched as Cade leaned forward. He nuzzled her breasts and stroked his nose back and forth on her turgid nipples. For reasons unknown to her, Yuki's hips pumped forward at the sensation. His lips replaced his nose and soon she was immersed in delicious tingles as he wrapped his lips around her puckered nipple. Cade swirled his tongue around the stiff bud, sneaking in soft flicks and Yuki lost it.

Her hips bucked uncontrollably, as she realized that there was a connection between her sensitive nipples and the secret place between her legs. A tension built there when he continued on to the other peak. Soon, Yuki thought that she would lose it if the tightness in her belly wasn't released.

Cade sensed her urgency and he wanted to make sure she reached her release. Before he caused the pain he knew would, when he breached her barrier. He placed his hand on Yuki's chest and gently applied pressure, guiding her to lie back in the soft grass. Cade lifted her soft thighs to rest on his broad shoulders.

Yuki's mound was covered in smooth ebony hair that laid against her pale skin. Cade could see how the blood pulsing in her sex had turned her labia into a pretty pink color. Her clit protruded from between them, begging for his attention. Droplets of water clung to her flesh and mingled with her arousal that glistened at her entrance. He glanced up at Yuki and she looked at him uncertainly.

"Cade, what are you doing?" Yuki asked reaching her hands down to cover her beautiful quim.

"Don't. Let me show you." Cade said as he moved her hands away from her swollen sex.

Yuki let her head fall back and squeezed her eyes closed in embarrassment. She had no idea what Cade was doing or why he wanted to put his face anywhere near her hidden places. Then she felt him rub his nose up her cleft and then blow gently against her feverish skin. Yuki cried out and shot forward. She gripped his hair in her hands and pulled his head away. Cade grinned up at her, smug satisfaction written all over his face.

"More?" He asked.

"Y-Yes!" She gasped.

Yuki laid back once more, now ready for his touch. Though nothing would've prepared her for what Cade brought out of her. He kissed and nibbled at her labia as he went up one side and down the other. Once he felt that she was prepared, Cade's mouth found the tight bundle of nerves between her lips and his tongue lapped at it greedily. Yuki's hips rose up to meet his decadent lips and tongue shamelessly, threatening to unseat him.

Cade latched onto her clit more firmly and circled his tongue around the hard nub. Her thighs clenched his head, her back arched, and she inhaled sharply. Then Yuki exploded. Her breath burst from her lungs in a melodic cry. Her thighs released his face and trembled violently.

Yuki felt rapturous, as if she was floating on a cloud. Though as her inner channel clenched and flexed, she craved more. She felt empty, she wanted to be filled. She didn't have to wait for long. Cade's need had reached a breaking point and Yuki found herself back in his arms as he lowered her back into the water.

Cade wrapped his arms around her waist, the tip of his aching manhood waiting at her entrance. He lowered her down further, dipping shallowly into her slick heat. Cade's gray gaze held Yuki's as he found her maidenhead. Her eyes widened and Cade pulled her towards him, capturing her mouth as he thrust through her hymen.

Yuki screamed into Cade's mouth and he swallowed the sound. The soothing warmth of the water helped to subside the sharp pain and quickly pleasure surged to the forefront again. Yuki felt full, finally getting what her body had craved that she didn't understand. She got it now and she didn't think she'd ever be able to go back. Her hands dove into his hair, pulling it from the leather tie. She held on tight to him as he pumped into her sensually. His gentle rhythmic thrusts built slowly. Then his control snapped and he moved to place her on the rock ledge again. Cade stepped up onto a natural stone step, placing him at the perfect position. He gripped her hips tightly and stroked into her smoothly. Yuki writhed in ecstasy and Cade increased his speed. He slammed into her until he felt her walls squeeze his bursting cock, tightly. Only to then release him with vigorous convulsions.

Yuki had tried to remain quiet, but the second climax exploded in powerful waves. An unexpected scream ripped from her throat as she dug her nails into Cade's strong forearms. He quickly pulled her back into his arms and continued to pump into her. Her wet, warmth and flexing muscles rent a violent orgasm and growl from him and his seed spilled deep in her womb.

Cade eased them back into the water as they clutched at each other tightly. He was overwhelmed by the amount of feelings he had for the little curvy princess. He felt that he could've stayed in that moment for all time. But then the sounds of swords being drawn woke him from his fantasy.

Both Yuki and Cade whipped their heads around to see seven samurais surrounding them with seven different expressions written on their faces. They ranged from downright furious to near hysterical laughter.

Cade quickly reached for his discarded jacket lying next to the pool and threw it over Yuki's shoulders, trying to shield her naked body from their eyes. Once he was done, Cade held up his hands in surrender.

Mortified, Yuki buried her face in Cade's neck. She wanted him to duck down into the water and never come up again.

"Princess, what is this?" Takashi asked angrily.

Yuki just shook her head quickly against Cade's neck, refusing to look up.

"Gentlemen, if we could have just a moment, we'd be glad to have this discussion when we're both decent." Cade suggested.

Takashi looked on with a disgruntled face, not wanting to back down. In the end, he gave in, if only for the princess' sake.

"Fine. But make it quick." He turned to walk away and then stopped to look back. "Meet me at the house." Then he stormed off with the six others trailing close behind.

Yuki and Cade reluctantly pulled apart and quickly dressed over their still wet bodies, not wanting to test the fearless leader of the village. They swiftly made their way back towards the village and Takashi's house. Neither noticed the naturally heated pool turn a bright glowing blue and the ethereal figure of water rising up to watch them.

"Yurei, has the huntsman found the princess and done what I've asked of him?" Empress Kasumi asked the watery figure in front of her.

"No, your Highness. First the huntsman destroyed the box for her heart and threw it in a river." The spirit informed Kasumi.

"What?!" The Empress bellowed, fury instantly radiating from her entire body.

"Yes, Empress. And I'm afraid there is more. Once he found her, he made love to her in one of the mountain springs. He told her of your plans and said that he had come to protect her." The translucent image of Kasumi said calmly, though calm is not what the woman, herself, was feeling.

"Fool! He's ruined everything! I'm so sick of men. Mindless rutting bastards! Only caring about the pricks between their legs." Kasumi screamed. "I'll do it myself. Yurei, I need to use the last of my power to disguise myself and once I get her heart, I'll be invincible. Please, help me." She requested.

"Empress, I must warn against this. If you lose the last of your powers and are unable to succeed in killing her, you will be irrevocably vulnerable." The spirit warned her.

"I will not fail." Kasumi said arrogantly. "Now change me and give me a deadly treat the princess won't be able to resist." The Empress smiled sinisterly as a blue glow surrounded her.

~~~

Yuki and Cade sat cross-legged, side by side as they held hands across from Takashi. Mai stood just outside the doorway wondering what had happened with the American. Takashi stared at them for several moments. Yuki was a bundle of nerves but Cade was stoic, never flinching under the weight of the samurai's gaze.

"Princess, I have no authority in how you conduct yourself. I am not the Emperor. However, I do feel responsible for your well-being. It is not proper for someone of your station to fornicate with some foreigner in the woods." Takashi scolded.

Mai clasped her hand over her mouth as she tried to silence her gasp of surprise at what Yuki had done.

"Don't berate her. It wasn't her fault." Cade spoke up, defending Yuki.

Takashi turned his cold gaze to the huntsman. "You dare lay your hands on the Princess of Japan?! Was that your purpose, to destroy her and her reputation?" His voice rose in anger.

"Neither. I was sent by the Empress to kill Yuki and bring back her heart." Cade said honestly to the loud gasp of Mai and the widening eyes of the samurai.

"Mai, you may come in. We know you're spying anyway." Takashi said, trying not to laugh.

The pretty maid came flying in and knelt next to Yuki, taking her hand firmly. "Princess, are you alright?" Mai said with worry.

"I'm fine, Mai." Yuki soothed her frazzled maid.

"So you didn't kill her as asked, but what you did was no better. Explain yourself!" Takashi said, not nearly finished with the discussion.

"Not that I feel that I have to, but I will out of respect for you, as the leader of this village." Cade prefaced before continuing. "Yuki and I have met before at the Imperial Palace. I fell in love with her that night." Yuki and Mai both gasped in shock, though Cade ignored them with a smirk and went on. "So I was surprised when I was summoned to the palace and commissioned to find and kill the princess. I could not let that happen. So I went in search for her, to protect her."

"And what of you desecrating her pure body?" Takashi pushed further.

"What of Mai's?" Yuki blurted out angrily. Both Mai and Takashi looked at her in surprise. "Yes, I saw you both together this morning as I left to go to the hot spring. I know Mai was a virgin before this morning. You desecrated her body, it's no different." Yuki said with her chin held high.

"But you're a princess! The standards are held higher for you." Takashi exclaimed.

"I don't care. I love him! And he is the first man that has ever shown interest in me. Is it better that I die a spinster than make my own choice to be happy?" Yuki argued back and Cade squeezed her hand in support.

"I'm sorry, Princess. I spoke out of turn. I meant no disrespect. I only want for you to be happy." Takashi inclined his head.

"Thank you." Yuki accepted his apology and then turned to more serious matters. "Now, do you plan on marring my dear Mai and make an honest woman of her?"

"I-I…" Takashi swallowed hard with the tables turned on him. "If she'll have me?"

Mai smiled shyly, but happily and nodded her head in agreement.

"What of him?" Takashi lifted his chin in Cade's direction. "Do you plan to marry the princess? Though remember, to marry a commoner or worse a foreigner means you lose your title, Princess." Takashi said earnestly.

"I know." Yuki said without regret.

"Are you sure?" Cade looked at her, searching her face for any doubt. "I don't want to ruin your life."

"That's impossible, since you're the one who's brought it to life." Yuki smiled bashfully.

"So you'll have me?" Cade asked unsure.

"For eternity, if I must." Yuki tried to make light of the heavy situation.

Cade chuckled before pulling Yuki into his arms and kissed her soundly. They began to get carried away, their tongues stroking against each other. All forgotten in the room besides themselves. Though a loud throat clearing, broke them apart and they looked up guiltily.

"Alright, an impromptu double wedding it is. We have two very important reputations to be upheld." Takashi announced as he stood up from the tatami mat.

Yuki, Cade, and Mai followed suit, unfolding from the straw woven floor. Mai walked over to her soon-to-be husband and bowed politely. Reserving their affections until they were in a more private setting. The rough edged American was having none of it. Cade pulled Yuki into his arms and again, kissed her deeply.

This time Takashi and Mai left the room. The village leader shook his head in exasperation and the loyal maid tried to reign in her giggles as they walked out, giving the oblivious couple much-needed privacy.

~~

The two brides-to-be took proper baths in the hot springs, and then helped dress each other for the evening ceremony. The women in the village found two of their best kimonos to lend to Yuki and Mai. Takashi and Cade wore the traditional groom's black and white ensemble. Takashi's hair was in a perfect Japanese top knot and Cade's was slicked back into a ponytail at the nape of his neck.

Both couples exchanged Japanese vows in front of the entire village. Afterwards, they enjoyed a spontaneous feast that had been quickly put together by the local women. Later that night, before Cade made love to Yuki, he haltingly exchanged the common Christian vows he knew.

He wanted to tie himself to her in every way possible. Through her people and traditions as well as his own. So that when he stroked into her, tying himself to her in the most intimate ways, he knew she was his for life.

~~~

    The next morning the village men and Cade went out on a celebratory hunting trip for the day. Cade left Yuki flushed and a little embarrassed after he kissed her soundly in front of the entire village, before riding away. Takashi left behind Shin and Masaru to protect the women in the village.

    Now that Yuki's status had been lowered to commoner with her marriage to Cade, she requested that she learn the ways of the villagers. So the women spent the day showing her how to tend the crops and other daily chores she hadn't been privy to learn in the palace.

    Evening was fast approaching and soon the men would be returning with the game they'd caught. Yuki and Mai had been working on dinner for their men, knowing they'd be starved when they arrived. Yuki stepped out to the entrance of Takashi's home to enjoy the fresh evening air and stretch her aching muscles. She wasn't used to the hard manual labor, though she enjoyed it.

    As she stood there, she saw a little old woman that she'd never seen before in the village. The woman pushed a cart of fresh produce and goods. The wheels to the cart got stuck in a rut and threatened to topple over. Yuki quickly ran over to assist and helped the old woman straighten the cart.

    "Thank you! Thank you so much, my dear." The old woman exclaimed. "You are so very kind." She gently patted Yuki's hand.

"It was my pleasure." Yuki brushed off the compliment.

"Here take this…as my way of saying thank you." The old woman held up the reddest apple Yuki had ever seen. Yuki looked in the old woman's eyes and felt a shiver of recognition run through her. Though she couldn't remember ever seeing the woman before. "Go on take it. It'll be the best apple you've ever tasted. I guarantee it." She coaxed further, holding it out closer for Yuki to take.

"Sure. Thank you." Yuki took the apple.

"Take a bite, my dear. Tell me what you think." The woman grinned brightly.

Yuki lifted the apple to her mouth. It was so unspoiled that she almost didn't want to bite into it to ruin its perfection. But she could see that the woman was anxious to see what she thought. So she bit down into the sweet fruit. As she chewed and swallowed, she thought it was the best fruit she had ever tasted.

Yuki started to speak but it felt like her airways were closing up. She began to choke and she reached for the woman as she fell to the ground, pleading for help with her eyes. She saw the old woman smile the most evil smile she had ever seen. Yuki's world started to go black, but she heard the woman's final words before the darkness took her. She knew she had made a dire mistake.

"Your heart is mine."

~~~

The men made their way over the last rise on the mountain road, into the village. They were in a jovial mood due to their successful hunt. Cade scanned the village looking for his bride, when he saw many of the villagers huddled around the front of Takashi's home.

Cade immediately spurred his horse into a trot towards the crowd and the other men followed. He jumped from his horse before it even stopped fully, when she saw Yuki crumpled on the ground. The crowd parted as he ran forward and he dropped to his knees in front of her. Cade lifted Yuki into his arms and he placed his ear against her chest, but heard only silence.

Tears of sorrow and rage ran down his face as he rocked her back and forth. Cade looked up in question at the people gathered around him, hoping for answers. Mai looked down at him while tears streamed down her face.

"What happened, Mai?" Cade asked in desperation.

"I don't know. I came out of the house to see what Yuki was doing and I saw her on the ground. I looked around and I saw an old woman quickly walking away as Masaru and Shin ran up to see what was wrong. They ran after her, heading in that direction." Mai pointed down the road leading further up the mountain.

Cade gently laid Yuki back down on the ground and ran back to his horse, jumping on smoothly. Takashi and the rest of the men quickly followed and they galloped off in the direction Mai pointed towards.

Rage filled every inch of Cade's body as he pushed his horse hard down the road. They quickly caught up to Shin and Masaru, who had given chase on foot.

"Where is she?" Cade said as they stopped next to the two panting men.

"We think she ran off, up through there." Masaru pointed up a steep incline.

Cade's eyes searched through the foliage and saw the bent and broken limbs of someone's swift and careless retreat. He jumped down from his horse and quickly followed the bread crumbs the woman left. Takashi hopped down as well and gestured for his men to follow.

Cade reached the top of the summit, barely winded as the thirst for vengeance gave him wings. He saw the old woman as she tried to climb up the side of the mountain. When she realized she was trapped, she faced him and the others defiantly.

"You ruined everything, huntsman! If you would've done the job I asked of you, I wouldn't have had to come do it myself." The woman screeched.

At her words, Cade realized who she was and recognized the Empress in the old woman's eyes. He drew his sword and Kasumi looked at him smugly.

"Do you think it matters if you kill me? It's already too late, the princess is dead!" She cackled at him.

Cade's rage blinded him and an anguished cry tore from his throat. He ran forward and cut the woman down with one blow of his sword. Kasumi barely had time to make a sound before her eyes rolled to the back of her head and she fell over the mountain face to her death. Though her death did little to soothe Cade's ache.

He and the men quietly made their way back to the village. A deep melancholy spread over them and only deepened as the men made their way back into the silent and mourning hamlet. The sun had dropped behind the mountain and the evening was fast approaching.

As they came closer, Cade could see that they had placed Yuki's lifeless body on a wooden platform surrounded by flowers. Villagers were coming up to her to pay their respects. Cade slowly slid down from his horse and reluctantly came forward, not wanting to say goodbye. The villagers stepped back to give him space.

"You look so beautiful." Cade said as a few tears slid down his face to land on her folded hands, resting on her stomach. "You don't even look dead. You're cheeks and lips still hold a hint of pink." He caressed the back of his hand down her soft cheek. "And you even still feel warm to the touch. I must be going mad in my desperation for you to stay with me." He choked out.

Cade laid his head on her hands and kissed her pale skin. He then moved up to her face and laid his lips, wet with tears on hers. He kissed her softly for a few beats. Then he broke the kiss and rested his forehead on her chest as he sobbed brokenly.

Fingers stroking his hair jarred him. Cade glanced down at her and saw Yuki looking up at him as she stroked his hair. His eyes widened in shock, thinking he must have died and was being reunited with her in heaven.

"Am I dead?" He asked her.

"No, I'm alive." Yuki smiled softly at him.

"How?" Cade asked in wonder.

"I don't know. Your love, maybe." Yuki suggested.

Cade really didn't care why, all he knew was that his world was once again right. He grabbed her shoulders and pulled her into his embrace. His lips found hers and once more kissed Yuki deeply in front of the entire village, propriety be damned.

Takashi, Mai and the rest of the villagers were so happy that Yuki was alive that they didn't care either and cheered them on. Cade broke away from the kiss and looked deeply into Yuki's mahogany colored eyes.

"Don't ever leave me again, do you hear me?" Cade said fiercely.

"Never."

~~~

So with the death of the evil Empress, Yuki's father swiftly recovered and reclaimed his throne. He was not happy that his beloved daughter's status had been lowered to commoner due to her marriage. Though, the light in Yuki's eyes and the love that radiated from Cade's, filled the Emperor with joy. He soon remarried to a demure woman and had the son Japan needed.

Yuki and Cade led a life of adventure between their two countries. Keeping their promise to never leave the other again.

••••

Wanderlust

*A*liyah Lane sat in a boardroom thousands of miles away from home, in the beautiful city of Amsterdam. She would normally be fighting jetlag, like every other trip she'd been on, around the world. But not today.

Her eyes were laser focused on Shayne Madden, the owner of the company she was doing consulting for. Aliyah thought that if she looked up 'silver fox' in the urban dictionary, Shayne's picture would more than likely be next to the definition. He was a panty-dropper for sure. He looked like Eric Dane, McSteamy from *Grey's Anatomy* with the accent of Jean Claude Van Damme. He was from Belgium and spoke French, Dutch, and English. Aliyah wondered what other talents he had with this tongue, besides languages.

Aliyah shook her head, trying to clear the haze of arousal and naughty thoughts from her mind. She had a job to do and fantasizing about her client wasn't going to get it done. Besides, when had she ever been a horny sex crazed person. *Never!* She thought to herself.

"What was that, Ms. Lane?" Shayne asked, watching her intently.

"Uh…nothing, Mr. Madden. Please continue." Aliyah said in mortification.

She wanted to slide down her chair and under the long table. She hadn't realized that she'd said her thoughts out loud. She had no idea what had come over her. Normally she was so straight-laced and composed. In fact, everyone who knew her, told her that she needed to relax more often. She needed to let loose and have fun every once in a while.

Aliyah agreed wholeheartedly. But she had been so reserved and conservative for so long, she didn't know how to unwind. She hadn't had sex in six years, for heaven's sake. She had turned forty a little over a week ago. She was unmarried, no boyfriend, and no prospects for one either. She was married to her career and was too uptight to have casual sex. She was a walking, talking stick in the mud.

The last boyfriend that she'd had, cheated on her with a girl that looked like a pornstar. Aliyah wanted to be angry, but in the end she couldn't even blame him. The sad part was, she hadn't even cried when she'd found out. She was dullness personified in the sack. Plus, she was so busy traveling around the world, helping companies expand to the States that she didn't have time to give a man any attention.

So, she was completely taken aback by her intense attraction to Silver McSteamy Fox. As he stood at the head of the boardroom table, speaking animatedly about his company with the most delectable accent. He was all tall, broad, blond-turned-silver with a little manly scruff on his face, bundle of sexiness. His amazing physique was covered in gray dress slacks and a dark blue fitted V-neck sweater. His silvery-blue, hooded and narrow eyes, zeroed in on Aliyah and held her gaze throughout most of the meeting.

"…which is why I'm hoping to expand to America." Shayne said with excitement.

His company, Mad Elegance, was a successful European furniture company. Shayne had built it from the ground up. He was a brilliant furniture designer and carpenter. His Dutch/Modern infusion was an instant sensation and orders for his pieces skyrocketed. He eventually had to expand to mass produce the furniture in a factory. He'd started his company at thirty-years-old and currently at forty-five, he was in the prime of his life and career. Now, he was looking to get the company name out to the States.

Aliyah mentally shook her head, to clear her scrambled thoughts about the gorgeous man. She then cleared her throat to begin her speech. "Well your numbers are good for the quarter. So I'm sure you can use some of the profits to start advertising in the States. But it probably won't be enough. We need to set up a crowdfunding campaign. You need to advertise on television, magazines and online. And don't underestimate social media. And just having an account on one, isn't enough. Get on all of them. *Instagram* would be perfect for your company. Post pictures of your beautiful furniture and people are going to want to know where they can get it. You may even want to open a few boutique stores in high-end areas, so people can come in and actually see and touch the furniture in person." Aliyah instructed and Shayne listened closely, as his staff wrote down her points. "I'll help you setup everything in the course of the next week that I'm here."

"I really appreciate you coming all the way here to help, Aliyah." Shayne said softly, his sincerity was written all over his face.

Though, all Aliyah heard was her name on his beautifully accented tongue. It sounded like satin over gravel, smooth and rough all at the same time. And she actually flushed like a schoolgirl, in response. *What is wrong with me?*

~~~

Shayne saw the flush creep up Aliyah's light, golden-brown skin. A wolfish grin spread across his face at her discomfiture. The moment she stepped into his offices and he'd shook her small, delicate hand, he had been entranced. The knockout curves she hid behind a well-tailored pantsuit, were made for sex. Her honey-colored skin and more than ample round ass would look lovely all pink from a good spanking. Her face was just as stunning as the rest of her. Large, downward slopped eyes…bedroom eyes that were chocolate brown and seductive. A straight full nose and deliciously plump lips.

Everything about her screamed sex goddess. Though Shayne was pretty sure that the lovely woman hadn't had a good fuck in a long time, if ever. Her posture and serious face said, "Keep your distance. Do not trespass." Shayne grinned inside at the challenge. He was fond of breaking the rules. And he couldn't think of anything better than cracking her hard exterior and bringing out the soft, seductive woman he knew was underneath.

He knew exactly where to do it… *Wanderlust.* …and who could help. *Nia would get a kick out of this tightly wound beauty.* Though, he knew he'd have to give it a few days to feel her out. He didn't want to extend an invitation, only to freak her out if she wasn't willing. He could tell she was skittish.

Be patient, Shayne.

~~~

Though Shayne couldn't be too patient, since he knew that Aliyah would only be in Amsterdam for a week. So, the next couple of days, he unleashed a subtle sensual assault on the unsuspecting woman. So much so, that Aliyah was not completely clueless to the attack, but had no idea how to respond.

Shayne seemed to be everywhere she went as she worked with his employees. The looks he gave her were definitely not what she would've called professional. He looked like a predator that had just found its next meal. When he was within touching distance, he always found a way to put his hands on her. Light pressure on her lower back, as he guided her into a room. A gentle touch on her hand, when he wanted to get her attention, instead of just saying her name. Tucking an imaginary tendril of hair behind her ear, that had supposedly come loose from her severe bun. During lunch one day, he even cupped her chin and brushed a crumb from the corner of her mouth with his thumb.

By Thursday, Aliyah was a bundle of frazzled nerves. The tension in her body had built up to the point that she thought she'd go mad. She was wound so tight that every time he came up to her, she jumped out of her skin. *I can't take much more of this.*

"Is everything alright, Aliyah?" Shayne asked, a knowing smirk spread across his face.

"I-I'm fine. Just a little tense, I guess." Aliyah admitted.

"Hmm…maybe you just need to unwind." Shayne suggested.

"That's not the first time someone has told me that." Aliyah closed her eyes and expelled a harsh breath.

"Then maybe it's time that you take the advice." Shayne said as he reached into the pocket of the black slacks he was wearing.

He pulled out a fancy red and gold embossed playing card. He held the card out to her. Aliyah just looked up at him in question.

"Go ahead. Take it." Shayne continued to hold the card in front of her.

Aliyah finally reached out to take the card with a shaky hand. She broke eye contact with his intense steel blue stare. Then she looked down at the card curiously. The playing card had two red Qs and hearts in diagonal corners and only one word was written in the middle in gold. *Wanderlust.* She flipped the card over and all that was there, was an address. Aliyah turned the card back over, thinking that there had to be more to it.

"What is it?" She asked confused.

"Come and find out." Shayne said vaguely.

"Well how should I dress? Is it a spa? A club? A restaurant? I know nothing about this place and no one that'll be there." Aliyah said trying to gather more information before she made an educated decision.

"Stop overthinking things. Just come. I'll be there at ten o'clock tonight. Bring the card with you because it's a private club and you can't get in without an invite. It's your golden key through the rabbit hole." Shayne informed her cryptically.

"Uh, okay." Aliyah said skeptically.

Shayne turned and started to walk out of her temporary office. He stopped in the doorway and turned back. He grinned when he caught her checking out his ass. Aliyah swallowed loudly.

He looked her sensible pantsuit, up and down before speaking. "One more thing. If you have one…wear a dress." Shayne recommended before walking out of the office.

Aliyah gulped nervously. She looked down at her navy blue suit with a frown. "What's so wrong with pantsuits?" She whispered to herself.

~~~

Several hours later, Aliyah looked at herself in the full-length mirror in her hotel room. She wore the only dress she had brought with her. She always brought one dress on her trips, just in case there was a business dinner or if she got the gumption to enjoy whatever city she was in. She never did. This was the first time she'd be breaking her routine.

"Okay, maybe this is better than a pantsuit." Aliyah conceded to her reflection.

The dress was all black with crystal beading on the plunging V-neckline. The bottom half of the dress stopped above her knees and fit like a second skin to her thighs, hips, and ass. It showcased her plump shapely legs, invitingly. The top half billowed out loosely, connecting to sleeves that stopped at her elbows, making them look like wings. The dress was definitely outside of her comfort zone, since one of her long-time friends had picked it out for her. It was very sexy, but classy enough for her to feel slightly at ease. She paired the dress with her sensible black pumps for work.

"You can take the girl out of the pantsuit, but you can't take the pantsuit out of the girl." Aliyah joked to herself.

She decided to redo her makeup for the evening. She gave herself a dramatic smoky eye and red lips. Aliyah also chose to wear her hair down for the evening. Her strict bun had created ebony waves in her hair and they fell to the middle of her shoulder blades.

Now that she was ready, she just had get up the courage to actually leave the room. Aliyah plopped down on her bed. She reached into her black clutch bag and grabbed the little playing card. The mysterious invitation. Deep in thought, she flipped it over and over again in her hands like she had done all day. She flopped back on the mattress and stared at the ceiling. She closed her eyes and took a deep fortifying breath.

~~~

Aliyah gave the cab driver the address to the establishment. It had taken her several minutes to be brave enough to leave the hotel and now she felt so nervous she could vomit. She was staying near one of the most popular areas in Amsterdam. Rembrantplein. It was a square that housed many clubs and cafes. Aliyah always made a point of staying in the most "happening" areas in whatever city she was staying in. Just in case she decided to actually live life. Though most times she just looked out the window at the activity below, while she ate her dinner and then went to bed alone.

The cab passed by the festivities now. Revelers where everywhere. The centuries old architecture passed by in a blur on one side and one of the many canals and bridges on the other. Soon they entered into the Red Light District and Aliyah looked wide-eyed at the women in the big picture windows. They displayed their ample delights to passersby, vying for new clientele.

A little past the famous district, the cabbie turned onto a nearly deserted street. He stopped the car in front of a beautiful stone building. A sign in muted gold read *Wanderlust* and the image of a playing card, hovered above the W. It was the queen of hearts.

Aliyah paid the cab driver and hesitantly got out of the car. She stood in the street for a moment, immobile. A car coming down the street honked at her and she jumped out of the way. Aliyah stepped up on the sidewalk and looked at the stairs that led down to an elegant red door. Above the archway to the door was written, Rabbit Hole. *I wonder if that was what Shayne had meant about the rabbit hole?*

She reached into her clutch and pulled out the white, red, and gold card. She slowly started her descent down the stairs. She raised her fist to the door to knock but the little door to a large peep hole opened, before Aliyah's hand could connect with the wood. A man's eyes stared at her through the hole.

"Your golden key, please?" The man asked.

Aliyah held up the card and his big paw snatched it from her through the peep hole.

"You're late." The man said to her through the door.

"Sorry, I..." She started to apologize. "Wait? How would you know I'm late?" Aliyah asked with a frown.

The man didn't reply. His only response was to open the door. Aliyah looked up at the big burly man, dressed in a black suit and tie. She thought that he kind of resembled a rabbit. Though she quickly forgot about the man as she looked into the building.

The door opened into a darkened spacious bar. The large room was painted a dark gold color and had massive and elaborate archways and pillars. Only some recessed lighting in red and gold, lit the space. Colorful bottles lined the back of the bar and plush red stools lined the front. Private alcoves wrapped around the perimeter of the room, furnished with large red couches. Heavy red drapes hung on the sides of each alcove. Some were open and others closed to give the occupants privacy.

Sharply dressed men and women mingled, holding quiet discussions. The low conversations blended together to create a low hum that reverberated through Aliyah's body. Some people were looking up at a few flat screen televisions mounted to the walls and pillars. Aliyah looked up to see what was on the TVs, and nearly choked on her own spit.

The televisions were displaying people in the throes of passionate lovemaking. Twosome, threesomes, and more. Aliyah's mouth flapped open and closed several times, which of course was how Shayne found her.

"Aliyah." He breathed softly as he grasped her hand and brought it up to his lips. "I'm so glad you could make it." Shayne said just above her hand, his breath ticking the fine hairs there before he touched his lips to her clammy skin.

"Th-The bouncer s-said I'm late." Aliyah stuttered, her knees quaking at the feel of his lips on her flesh.

"You are." He said with a sexy grin as he straightened up again.

"How would he know that?" She asked perplexed.

"Because I told him you'd be coming and what you looked like. Though I must say, I didn't even come close to describing you well enough. You're stunning!" Shayne complimented.

Aliyah only flushed in response, words unable to pass her lips.

"Come, have a drink with me." Shayne said as he guided her towards the bar. His fingers at the small of her back.

Aliyah trembled at the touch of his hand through the fabric of her dress. While Shayne ordered their drinks, he kept his hand low on her back and lightly stroked up and down the lower curve of her spine with the back of his fingers. It was subtle, but his seduction had begun.

"Let's make a toast." Shayne suggested, holding up his champagne flute. "To…new adventures." He grinned broadly as their glasses clinked.

As Aliyah quietly sipped the champagne he had ordered for them, she tried to covertly take in his sexy appearance. He wore black dress slacks and shining black shoes. A pristine white dress shirt was tucked into the slacks and a beautiful deep blue tie was around his neck. Over the shirt was a fitted black vest that emphasized his broad chest and narrow waist. Around each arm were two vintage-style, casino dealer black armbands that wrapped around his impressive biceps. And to finish off the whole sexy stylish look, he wore a black newsboy hat over his short silver locks.

Shayne's eyes were practically glowing arctic blue, as he gazed at her from under his dark hat. Aliyah watched as he took the hat off and stuffed it in one of the back pockets of his pants. Then he downed the rest of his champagne, never taking his eyes off of her the entire time.

"Let me show you around. And I want to introduce you to someone." Shayne said, as he took her empty glass and set it on the bar before leading her towards a red door in the back of the room.

"T-There's more?" Aliyah said nervously.

"So much more." Shayne's deep gravelly voice said seductively.

He opened the door and drew her into the cavernous room. Aliyah stood in shock at the sight that greeted her. She finally understood where the footage of the people on the TVs in the bar were coming from.

All types of couples were in different states of dress or undress, all around her. All of them in different stages of lovemaking and on several kinds of apparatuses. Couches, cushioned benches, wooden Xs with leather cuffs at each end, and so on. Built against the wall was a type of tool rack, but the tools that adorned it were of the sensual torture variety.

The room was decorated in dark colors and only some soft low lighting lit the area. Sultry background music set the mood and fought for dominance over the moans, groans, skin smacking and other sounds of sex.

Aliyah was appalled and aroused all at the same time. She wasn't quite sure whether she was more appalled by what she was seeing or her reaction to it. Her eyes grew wide, her pulse raced at her neck, her skin became flushed and damp, her stomach churned with the release of a storm of butterflies, and her sex flooded with moisture.

Shayne watched Aliyah intently, trying to gauge her reaction. He saw a tinge of pink on her cheeks. A light sheen of sweat broke out on her brow. And her ample breasts rose and fell harshly as if she'd run a marathon. *Oh, the marathon hasn't even begun, les amoureux.*

"What is this place?" Aliyah whispered shakily.

"A place for you to unwind. To be yourself. To explore your baser needs. This is a whole world, I bet you didn't even know existed." Shayne said softly against her ear.

Aliyah just swallowed in response.

"Here comes someone I want you to meet." Shayne told her.

Aliyah watched as a stunning woman glided towards them. She had to be one of the most beautiful women Aliyah had ever seen. She was also black, but her coloring and bone structure hinted that she was from Africa. Her skin was like flawless, smooth black onyx, wrapped in a red leather corset and skintight black leather pants. She was tall and slender with a glorious afro framing her striking face. Her strong, confident demeanor and high cheekbones reminded Aliyah of Grace Jones. She was instantly intimidated. The riding crop she held didn't help either.

"Who is this lovely creature you have brought into our ranks, Shayne?" The gorgeous woman asked in a beautiful accent Aliyah couldn't quite place.

"This is Aliyah. Aliyah, I'd like to introduce you to our esteemed hostess, Nia. The queen of hearts, herself." Shayne gave the introductions.

"N-Nice to meet you, Nia." Aliyah's voice trembled.

"Oh, what a tense little thing, you are!" Nia tsked as she pulled Aliyah further into the room. "We must do something about that."

Aliyah looked back at Shayne as he followed close behind. A Cheshire cat smile spread across his face. The smile screamed trouble and she shivered in anticipation.

Nia stopped in front of an empty, large wooden X and Aliyah looked at in trepidation. Both Nia and Shayne circled around her a few times, as if they were sizing her up. To predators circling their prey.

"Um…if this is supposed to be relaxing, you might want to rethink your business plan." Aliyah said fearfully, her eyes following them as they stalked her.

They both chuckled before Nia spoke again. "We're just thinking of the best way to begin. Be patient, my dear." She then turned to Shayne. "I think a blindfold would be best. So she won't freak out by what's coming next."

"Hmm...I agree." Shayne spoke thoughtfully.

"Uh, won't I freak out more *not* knowing what's happening?" Aliyah's eyes widened even further at the thought.

"At first, yes. But once you begin to trust him, it'll become easier." Nia explained.

Aliyah looked to the man in question and he nodded slightly. His silvery blue eyes never moved from her, like there were no naked people having sex in the room. His jaw flexed and his hands were fisted tightly at his sides, the only indications that he was doing everything in his power to restrain himself. And a telltale bulge pressed snuggly against the zipper of his slacks.

"W-What is your p-part in this?" Aliyah said to Nia after she tore her eyes from Shayne's.

"I'm the Dominatrix, or Domme if you will, of the club. Mostly, I oversee the...*activities* of the club. I make sure that no one is taking things too far or abusing the rules. *And* I also help things along if someone is feeling...*hesitant*." Nia said meaningfully.

"W-What are the rules?" Aliyah couldn't seem to keep her voice from quivering.

"Well, that the submissives are willing, no one is pushed or hurt beyond their threshold, that anyone that comes into this room has adhered to the two drink maximum, and the club is kept secret." Nia ticked off.

"And I'm a s-submissive?" Aliyah asked in disbelief.

"Oh, so much more than you know." It was Shayne that finally spoke up. "Now, I think you've got the gist of it." He stepped close to her. "This is a place where you can let go. Let go of the bullshit of the outside world. Relinquish control and everyday life decisions, to me. It's my job to take the weight of the world off your shoulders and to gain your complete trust. In return, I'll give you more pleasure than you've ever known." His silky smooth accent wrapped around Aliyah like a warm blanket.

"O-Okay." She practically panted.

"I must follow the rules, so let's get the first rule out of the way. Do I have your permission to play?" Shayne asked seriously.

"Mmhmm," was all that Aliyah could get out as she nodded her head.

"Good. Now on to the next rule. I need a word from you that you'll use if I take things too far. A safeword," Shayne said.

"Teapot." Aliyah picked the first word that came to mind. *Really?!*

Shayne grinned.

Aliyah watched as Nia went to the wall and chose a black blindfold, medieval looking clamps and a soft leather flogger. She then placed them under a machine, flipped a switch and a bright blue light shined on the items. After a few minutes, she came back and handed the flogger and clamps to Shayne. She brought the blindfold over to Aliyah.

"We sanitize all of our toys with UV light, before and after each use. Just so you know that we keep things clean here. Now, close your eyes." Nia instructed.

Aliyah obeyed, even as she saw curious onlookers stop their lovemaking to watch her. Her body trembled as everything went black, when Nia placed the blindfold over her face. She felt a soft kiss on the corner of her mouth and she realized it was Nia, when she spoke again.

"Just relax. Shayne will take good care of you." Nia whispered against Aliyah's mouth.

Aliyah felt a fingertip at her chin and she raised her face as the finger applied pressure upward. "I won't hurt you. You can trust me. I've waited for this since you first came into my office." Shayne's breath touched her lips.

She felt his firm lips on hers and she kissed him back softly. His warm tongue caressed the crease of Aliyah's mouth, asking for access inside. She obliged and opened her lips on a sigh. His tongue plundered her willing mouth. He stroked her tongue aggressively and Aliyah responded shyly. Shayne groaned at her hesitant strokes.

Aliyah was shocked by the passion he unleashed with just a kiss. She could not remember a time when a kiss made her feel so wanted. So desired.

Shayne released her lips and moved down to her chin. He nipped the skin there with his teeth, and she felt it in her gut. His tongue flicked and caressed its way down her jaw to her neck. His hands gripped her hips and slid around to her backside. He pulled Aliyah into him and she felt his hard bulge against her tummy. Aliyah whimpered with need.

"Shh… Soon, mon amour." Shayne soothed her.

"W-What d-does that mean?" Aliyah stuttered as he slowly inched her dress up her thighs.

"My lover." Shayne whispered in her ear and then flicked his tongue against the outer shell.

"Oh God!" Aliyah's knees buckled.

Never in all her life had she been so turned on. Aliyah had thought that she was dull or prudish, but in reality, she realized that she'd just had the wrong partners. And Shayne was only getting started.

Shayne backed away slightly and gradually drew the dress the rest of the way, up and over Aliyah's head. She instantly crossed her arms over herself and he stepped close to her again as he passed her discarded dress to Nia.

"Don't hide. You have a beautiful body. And it was made to be worshipped by me." Shayne said softly as he grasped her wrists and pulled her hands from her body.

Shayne kissed each of her shoulders before he pulled down the straps of her black bra. He kissed her forehead and nose as he reached behind her back and unclasped the lacy material. He took her clutch purse from her trembling hand, then peeled the bra slowly from her body and tossed them both to Nia. Shayne's hands cupped her heavy D-cup sized breasts. Her areolas were large and dark chocolate tipped. Unable to resist, he kissed down her neck to her beautiful breasts. He rubbed his lips over the soft nubs and they immediately tightened in response.

    He wanted her so badly, he thought that he'd lose his mind. But he knew he had to exercise some restraint if he wanted to make sure that she found her pleasure before he did. So, Shayne stood up straight and moved towards her, walking her backwards to the St. Andrew's cross. Once her back touched the wood, he grasped her left wrist and pulled it up to the first cuff. He held her hand there as Nia secured the leather cuff. Then they did the same with her right wrist.

    Now that her arms were secure, Shayne moved to her last article of clothing. He took his index finger and slowly stroked it down her neck to her sternum, through the middle of her luscious breasts, down her quivering tummy to the matching black lace boyshorts covering her mound. He traced his finger around the waistband of the panties and Aliyah trembled. Shayne turned his hand until his palm was flush with the lace, and his fingertips pointed down towards her sex. He slid his hand down further and cupped her heat. He could feel just how wet she was through her panties.

    Shayne gripped the material and tore it from her. Aliyah gasped as she was left naked, with the exception of her black heels. He brought the soaking wet panties up to his nose and breathed in her spicy scent. He tucked the panties into his pants pocket and then crouched down in front of her. Shayne lightly tapped her right foot and she lifted it for him. He pulled her ankle over to the cuff below and strapped her in, and then did the same with the other ankle. She was officially his, at least for the rest of the night.

    Shayne stepped back and took in her naked form and bit his lip hard. She was stunning. Her body was soft and supple. The term brickhouse came to mind as he gazed at her. The V between her thick thighs was embellished by a dark trim little triangle that directed the eye to her pretty pussy. Her caramel skin gleamed, only marred by the faint lines of stretch marks that adorned her hips and lower abdomen. Marks that told a story. Her story. Aliyah's tongue nervously wet her lush lips as she awaited his next move. Shayne unbuttoned each of the cuffs on his sleeves and then rolled them up to his elbows. *Time to go to work.*

Shayne was great with his hands, and for more than just building beautiful furniture. They were also for building up tension in a lovely woman and bringing her to a life-changing climax. Both skills came in handy and were talents he took very seriously.

He stepped up to Aliyah once more. He made sure that no part of his body was touching her as he leaned forward. Shayne kissed her lips, feather light and she surprised him by flicking her tongue against his lips. He growled deep in his throat, clutched her face in his hands, and deepened the kiss. Their tongues danced together and he mimicked with every dip of his tongue, what he would do to her later.

Shayne released her lips on a gasp and balled his hands into tight fists. He felt his control slipping and he wasn't even closed to done. It was time to move on to the next step in his sensual assault. And he was nothing, if not methodical.

"Aliyah, tell me one more time. What is your safeword?" Shayne asked.

"Teapot," she breathed.

"Mmm…good girl. Are you ready?" He asked.

"Y-Yes. No. I-I don't know. I'm nervous." Aliyah answered honestly.

"You're only nervous because this is all unknown to you. Let me educate you." Shayne said as he bent down and flicked his tongue against her nipple.

"Ahh! Yes!" Aliyah cried out and pulled at her restraints.

Shayne softly swirled his tongue around her nipple, then he clamped his lips around it and pulled gently. The coffee colored tip wrinkled and hardened further. Once he felt it was hard enough, Shayne held out his hand to Nia and she handed him the nipple clamps. He opened one of the clamps and then eased it closed over her hard peak. Aliyah gasped at the pinch of the clamp.

"It's okay, baby girl. There is a thin line between pain and pleasure and I'm going to take you to that line but I promise not to cross it. It'll make your pleasure that much better." Shayne informed her. "Are you alright?" He asked just to be sure.

"Uh huh." She nodded briskly, her chest heaving.

Shayne quickly moved to her other breast and gave it the same attention. This time Aliyah knew what was coming, though she still panted at the pinch. The pain didn't last very long and a slight numbness came over her nipples. Then, several seconds ticked by and nothing happened. She had no idea what he planned next and then her body shuddered as the soft fringes of the flogger caressed her body.

Shayne slowly tickled her skin with the fringes and she gasped. Then she felt nothing. But she heard the faint sounds of the flogger, as if he was whirling it round and round. She could even feel the slight breeze the twirling flogger made. Suddenly, she felt the light smack of the soft, thin tassels.

"Oh my God!" Aliyah shouted out.

It didn't hurt, but it was unexpected and made her skin tingle. Shayne started out slowly, making his way down from her breasts to her calves. When the fringes hit her labia and clit her back arched off of the cross. Then the smacks became a little firmer and quicker as he rained them down upon her flesh in random spots on her body.

The more he did this, the more blood rushed to the surface of her skin, making her skin hypersensitive. Aliyah's clit was so swollen with arousal, she could feel the pulse of her heartbeat in the tiny nub. Her thighs were slick from the dew that dripped from her cleft. A thin sheen of sweat covered her body.

Aliyah wasn't ready to say 'teapot' because of pain per se, but because she needed release somehow. She couldn't explain the feeling of wanting desperately for the torture to stop, but never wanting it to end either. She felt like one big exposed nerve.

"Shayne, please!" She begged as she pulled on her restraints.

The soft smacks stopped, immediately followed by his unexpected mouth on her folds. Aliyah inhaled sharply. Shayne licked up her cleft and flicked her clit ever so slightly, striking gold. Right at detonation, someone pulled the clamps from her nipples and the blood rushed back to them. A soft wet tongue flicked one of her nipples at the same time Shayne teased her sensitive button. Her hands fisted around the chains of her manacles, her back arched off of the cross, and a loud scream ripped from her throat.

Aliyah fell apart. Her hips pumped towards Shayne's awaiting tongue. She fucked his face with abandon, not caring about anything in that moment. Her thighs shook convulsively and her chest heaved with every harsh breath, pushing her breast further into the unknown mouth. She assumed that it was Nia. She never thought about being with a woman or letting one touch her, but she didn't care. Nothing mattered, except for the pleasure coursing through her.

Shayne's mouth disappeared from her weeping sex and the mysterious mouth moved to her other breast. After a few moments, Aliyah felt hands on one of her ankles, freeing her. Then the next was also freed and strong arms wrapped around her thighs. One minute she was empty and aching. The next she was lifted off her feet and impaled, with what felt like an enormous cock. He filled every inch of her in one powerful thrust. And Aliyah screamed again.

"Please…let me see you!" Aliyah cried as he continued to stroke into her smoothly.

Shayne reached up and pulled away the blindfold. Aliyah squinted as the light hit her eyes. Once they adjusted, she looked at his handsome face, focusing on his intense steel blue gaze. His jaw was slack and mouth open as hard pants escaped his lips, his warm breath fanning her face. She realized that he was completely naked and assumed he'd taken off his clothes after her first shattering climax.

The arm wrapped around her waist, clasped her tighter as he reached for the leather cuff and released her arm. Shayne reached for the other and released it too. Aliyah immediately dug her fingers in his short-cropped, silver hair.

Shayne carried her over to a plush red leather bench. He released her and positioned her on her knees, over the bench. His hand came down suddenly and smacked one ridiculously round cheek and as she clenched in surprise and he drove into her from behind. Aliyah's legs instantly began to quiver as he hit her G-spot and a new, startling orgasm radiated through her. Shayne didn't stop, even as her fluttering pussy drove him insane. He continued to plunder her deep recesses and one orgasm rolled into another.

Aliyah's arms could no longer hold her up and she collapsed, her ass still in the air. Shayne swiveled his hips and rained light slaps to her ass that ripple with every pump and sent electric pulses to her clit. Her cries could be heard throughout the entire room. Aliyah had never been vocal, but then again she hadn't had a reason to be. Shayne brought out the goddess in her.

The sex god himself, pulled out of her aching core. He lifted her from the bench and laid down on his back, his intentions clear. He wanted her to straddle him. It was the first opportunity Aliyah had to look at his magnificent cock. It was incredibly long and thick and harder than any erection she had ever seen. She attributed it to the silver cock ring that was nestled at the base of his well manscaped shaft.

In fact, she hadn't gotten a chance to see any of his naked body. All of him was a sight to behold. Corded arms with surprising tattoos. A defined chest with flat pink nipples, cut abs, and strong powerful legs. Michelangelo's David had nothing on this man.

Aliyah did as his eyes asked and she straddled his hips. Slowly, she slid down his hard length once more. She was so sensitive that she didn't know how much more she could take. Aliyah placed her hands on his hard chest for balance and used her legs to slide up and then back down his stiff manhood. She threw her head back as he went incredibly deep.

Shayne reached up and cupped her large breasts. He knew he was in trouble. In one evening he had become irrefutably addicted to this caramel temptress. He'd thought that it would've taken a couple of tries to break down her walls and pull her out of her shell. But her defenses crumbled under his assault. Her inner goddess must have been right there at the surface, waiting for someone who cared enough to break her free.

Shayne was ready to take back control. He braced her back as he flipped her onto her back on the bench. He lifted her legs up to her chest, position his cock at her slick entrance and dipped shallowly. Aliyah writhed beneath him.

"Shayne, I-I can't take much more." She panted out, her head lolling back and forth as if she was delirious.

He growled deep in his throat and began to stroke into her with demanding blows. Once more, her inner walls started to quake. Aliyah's back arched off of the bench, this time Shayne covered her mouth with his and captured her cries of release. And finally he let go. He came with an explosion. Shayne relinquished her lips and shouted out as jet after jet of cum pumped from him.

"Ahhh…f-fuck!" Shayne roared.

He continued to stroke into her slowly as he kissed Aliyah all over her flushed face. His semen still jetting from his still hard shaft. It was the hardest he had ever climaxed.

"Aliyah…" He breathed her name like a benediction. "You were magnificent."

"Me?" Aliyah asked, exhausted.

"Yes, you." Shayne confirmed.

He kissed her deeply. When he released her lips and looked up, Nia was grinning widely at him and the rest of the club members looked at them hungrily. *Sorry folks, we're not sharing.* Shayne looked back down at Aliyah and realized she had fallen into a deep oblivious sleep.

"I'll take care of you, mon amour." Shayne whispered.

~~~

Aliyah's eyes opened to the pale light of dawn coming through the window. She squinted as her eyes adjusted. As her eyes came into focus, the ceiling she was staring at looked very familiar. She sat up quickly and looked around at her surroundings. Aliyah was back in her hotel room.

"How did I…?" Aliyah started, but let the question hang in the air. "Holy shit! Was that all just a dream? Did I never even leave my room last night?"

She fell back on the bed again as she replayed the evening in her mind. *I just don't know.* Aliyah balled up her hands into tiny fists and hit the mattress a few times in frustration.

"I knew it was too good to be true!" She growled.

She looked over at the nightstand to see what time it was, knowing she needed to get ready for work. *How am I going to face Shayne after a dream like that?* Her eyes lit on something that sat by her phone. She got up on her hands and knees and crawled over to the bedside table. Aliyah reached for the playing card that sat on the table and read what it said just as there was a knock at the door.

The white card with gold lettering said, *Cum again...* Wide-eyed, she dropped the card and went to the door.

"Who is it?" Aliyah asked.

"Aliyah, its Shayne." The deep voice answered.

Aliyah opened the door to the gorgeous man. Before she could say anything, she was wrapped up in his warm, solid embrace. His lips devoured hers as he walked her backwards into the room and kicked the door closed.

"I couldn't wait to see you again." Shayne spoke between kisses.

"Then it wasn't a dream?" Aliyah asked against his lips.

"If it was, I don't ever want to wake up." Shayne answered sweetly.

"What about work?" She asked as he kissed down her neck.

"Fuck work. I own the place." He growled.

Aliyah and Shayne tumbled onto the bed in a tangle of limbs, lips, and urgent tongues. Aliyah's mind consumed with thoughts of a possible new foreign address, as Shayne's tried to figure out how he could convince her to stay. Their trip down the rabbit hole, just beginning…

~The End~

Acknowledgments

I'd like to thank Nadia, Sammy, and Essence for beta reading for me. Thank you so much for your thoughts, corrections and suggestions. I also want to extend my gratitude to Takae, for helping me with the kanji for *Snow White*. Otherwise, who knows what the kanji I would've used would have meant.

Also, I have to give a big shout out to the bloggers out there that have been invaluable to me in this process of promoting. Musings of an IR Romance Junkie, BrazenBabes, Romance Writer's Rodeo, Romance Between the Covers, and Rebirth of Lisa. You lovely ladies have helped spread the word about my work and I can't thank you enough!

I am also incredibly happy to have connected with some amazing authors that have been so helpful. You all gave a shoulder to lean on, kind ear to vent to, or precious advice/instructions. Kim Golden, Ines Johnson, Ruby Madden, Ava Mallory, and Harper Miller. I hope I didn't forget anyone.

I want to thank Taria Reed for her ahhhhhmazing cover design! I'm just tickled pink over this cover and often find myself staring at it. Ha! And thank you Kevin Saldutti and Sharifa Edwards for modeling so beautifully for the cover. Holy hotness you two are!!!

To my loyal readers…I freakin' love you ladies! You've made very difficult part of this journey, totally worth it. Your kind words breathe life into my frazzled brain. Thank you!!!

And as always, much love to my family and friends for being there for me as constant support and encouragement. I couldn't do any of this without you. Plus, many of you have been or will be used as characters in my books at some point. Incognito, of course.

I love you all!

About the Author

Twyla Turner currently resides in Arizona. She was born and raised in Joliet, Illinois. A Midwest girl at heart, though constantly moving from place to place, and always thinking of where she wants to go next. Having been an avid romance novel reader since junior high and minoring in Creative Writing. She felt that it was finally time to start combining her love of travel and writing, as well as her life experiences and putting them down on "paper". Which experiences, she'll never tell…well maybe, if you ask nicely.

Other books by Twyla Turner

The Struck Series:
Star-Struck
Awe-Struck

Damaged Souls Series:
Scarred
Open Wounds
Healed

THR3E

Love in the Wild

Connect with Author

Website:
www.twylaturner11.wix.com/novelswithcurves

Follow me:
Facebook: www.facebook.com/twylaturner11
Twitter: @TwylaTurner11
Instagram: https://instagram.com/novelswithcurves/

Meet the Cast of Curvy Ever After:
Pinterest: https://www.pinterest.com/twylite11/curvy-ever-after-the-cast-other-stuff/

Sign up for Twyla's newsletter Novels with Curves to get the latest updates and giveaways.
http://eepurl.com/btKLMf